ABOUT THE AUTHORS

ELEN LEWIS
Writer, ghostwriter, editor, author, writing trainer. Former journalist.
Editor of 26 and The Marketing Society. Books about brands and
babies. Novel about lightning. Mother like Iris.

JOHN MITCHINSON
Writer, publisher, pigkeeper. Co-founder of Unbound.
Director of Research for *QI*. Co-author of the *QI* books. Bearded.
Tweed clad. Man of Tew. Mouthpiece for Davey Mackintosh.

MARK WATKINS
After twenty years as an in-house corporate communications
professional, Mark became a freelance consultant and corporate
writer in 2008. He lives in Roskilde, Denmark, which didn't
prevent him channelling a Scottish PC.

JULIAN STUBBS
International brand strategist, writer and presenter living in
Stockholm, Julian Stubbs of Cloud Based Agency UP THERE,
EVERYWHERE wrote the part of Dr Simpson.

CLAIRE BODANIS
Enjoyed an imaginary life as Philip while writing the novel; in the
real world does most of her writing while running copywriting and
communications consultancy Falcon Windsor.

JOHN SIMMONS
Author, trainer, brand consultant. Educator/learner. Dark Angels and
26 co-founder. Books on writing for business. Occasional novelist/poet.
Nothing like his character Richard (please).

ANDY MILLIGAN
I've written five business books, started two businesses, have one
wife, two kids, and spent forty years supporting Plymouth Argyle.
I wrote Julia.

ROGER HORBERRY

I'm a copywriter, trainer and author responsible for the part of Robin 'Wastrel' White. If only my life were as colourful as my character's.

PAUL REDSTONE

Author, copywriter, brand builder and tech lover who is happiest when there is no signal. Far more mature than Rebecca. In years anyway.

MARTIN LEE

Branding specialist, co-owning small marketing business, Acacia Avenue. Writes for a life, not a living, especially the collaborative style of 26 and Dark Angels. Wrote Solomon.

JONATHAN HOLT

Wrote Callum. Studied creative writing at Goldsmiths. His stories have appeared in *Tell Tales* and *Goldfish*. By day, he writes for business.

STUART DELVES

Playwright, poet, copywriter. Co-founder of Dark Angels and Henzteeth. Creative collaborator with artists, film-makers, designers, illustrators. Cecil Ryan cameo.

ELISE VALMORBIDA

Author of *Matilde Waltzing*, *The Book of Happy Endings*, *The TV President* and *The Winding Stick*. Producer of award-winning indie Britfilm *SAXON*. And Adarsh.

SUSANNAH HART

I'm a brand consultant based in London. I'm also Chair of Governors at a local primary school and I write poetry. I wrote Stella.

JAMIE JAUNCEY

I'm a Scottish novelist, business writer and Dark Angels co-founder, based not a million miles from Balmore and Angus's native patch.

KEEPING MUM

KEEPING MUM

A novel by the

DARK ANGELS COLLECTIVE

unbound

This edition first published in 2014

Unbound

4–7 Manchester Street, Marylebone, London, W1U 2AE

www.unbound.co.uk

Typesetting and cover design by Sam Gray
Art direction by Mecob

A CIP record for this book is available from the British Library

ISBN 978-1-78352-041-1 (*special*)
ISBN 978-1-78352-040-4 (*trade*)
ISBN 978-1-78352-039-8 (*ebook*)

Printed and bound in India by
Replika Press Pvt. Ltd.

FOR ALL DARK ANGELS

CHARACTERS IN ORDER OF APPEARANCE

IRIS WHITE
The mother

DAVID MACKINTOSH
The host at Balmore

PC LACHLAN
The local policeman

DR SIMPSON
The local GP

PHILIP
A young guest at Balmore

RICHARD WHITE
Iris's elder son

JULIA WHITE
Richard's wife

ROBIN WHITE
Iris's younger son

REBECCA WHITE
Iris's teenage daughter

SOLOMON WHITE
Iris's husband

CALLUM CATTANACH
The local undertaker's stepson

CECIL RYAN
Owner of a hotel in the Lake District

ADARSH
Chef at a hotel in the Peak District

STELLA
Iris's friend at Oxford

ANGUS
An old friend of Solomon and Iris

Day 1

SATURDAY

IRIS

They say you should walk towards the light. Well I didn't. I fled. I ran away from it. I pushed the light back and it splintered in my hands like glass. I thought I might be dead because there was no blood. I raged, I wept. I shouted. There was no pain. I screamed. There was no noise. It wasn't time. It wasn't right. But still, I did not know that I was dead. Still, I hoped that I was not. I wasn't ready.

So now from a distance I must watch this private life of mine unfurl, spilling secrets over the children, over Solomon, like a rose bruised in a storm. I never intended to hurt them with the truth. I believe in the power of secrets. I believe that they can protect the ones you love. I believe that secrets can hold you down to earth when all you want to do is fly away.

When Rebecca was a newborn baby and the boys were at school, day and night swam together. I would lie beside her in a darkened room, inhaling the top of her head, listening for the lengthening of quick, shallow breaths. Her puckered, jerky hands clasping my index finger. I wondered if she could hold us together. If she would be enough, this tiny life of ours?

Later, I learned that children can also rip you apart. They can stand in between you, block out the light, drown out the words, mop up the love. Rebecca wasn't about us, or our love or our hope. She was the shape of love. That was all. The empty shape of love, dangling by a thread, swinging and twisting. And she couldn't make us whole. Nobody could.

There is a symbiotic association in the plant world called mycorrhiza. Such a satisfying word, sounding like the clearing of a throat. The plants give sugars to the fungus, the fungus gives nutrients to the plants. Most plants can't grow without their fungus, their roots are wrapped in each other. I never had that with Solomon. We didn't want each other, didn't even need each other. I thought I didn't need anybody. But I was wrong.

Her eyes were open.

It is always a shock, even when it's expected, which this was not. She'd seemed fine the night before, a little distracted but not unwell. She'd helped herself, as she always does, to a dram from the hall cabinet. The Macallan is her favourite, even though I've counselled her against it over the years. Too sweet and too popular down south, I would tell her. Try a Mortlach or one of the older Dalwhinnies. Much better balance and a longer finish.

I went up after breakfast, noting that her haggis – Macsween's, she always insisted – was untouched on the sideboard. I knocked and called her name softly through the door. Nothing. And there she was, absolutely still, staring into the semi-darkness. No sign of distress or panic. Her clothes from the night before hanging against the wardrobe; her toiletries lined up neatly on the bathroom shelf. I quickly left, went downstairs and called the police and left a message for Dr Simpson. A heart attack? Stroke? There will doubtless need to be a post mortem. Let's hope it's speedy. I'm guessing Cattanach's will come for the body. Balmore is fully booked this weekend, and nobody likes to think about dying on holiday. I know it's a common enough occurrence, particularly in large hotels. But Balmore isn't large, and, despite what everyone thinks, it isn't a hotel. It's a family house, which we choose to open up to strangers.

The essential calls made, I went back upstairs. I don't know how long I sat there next to her. What I felt was more puzzlement than sadness. The utter stillness of the dead is always disconcerting. And the random suddenness of death's arrival. I remembered the lines we used to recite at school: *Madam Life's a piece in bloom, Death goes dogging everywhere: She's the tenant of the room, He's the ruffian on the stair.* The ruffian has claimed many victims on the ancient staircases of this house. Four hundred years of sowing and reaping have filled its corridors with ghosts. But I did not expect death to visit this morning, as I walked down from the hill with the March sun in my eyes and the cock grouse's cries cascading down the glen.

I did not expect it and will not make it welcome.

A four-wheel drive had hit a stag and I could smell blood in the air. Plasticky, sickly.

'Venison for tea?' shouted one of the orange bibs who were sweeping loose wreckage from the road. I ignored the question and the other broom-handlers chuckled without breaking their rhythm.

The beast lay crumpled in the ditch at the roadside. I pictured him as he should have been, standing majestic on his hillside, surveying his realm. Then the radio burst through again and snapped me back into the moment.

Another death. Aye, aye. There'll be paperwork to be done tonight.

'PC Lachlan received. On my way.'

It's a bleak place, right enough, this part of Scotland. Wilderness tamed only by a narrow ribbon of road and rail. The rest is pretty much as it has always been. I wonder if the stag had just been unlucky, or whether he was making a stand of it – to remind us.

It's a bugger to find, the old house. It sits on a hill above what we still call 'the new road'. But the access road is easy to miss and I overshoot it.

A U-turn and a bit of swearing later and I'm bouncing up the unmade road before crunching to a stop on the gravel forecourt of Balmore House.

Mackintosh, the owner, is quickly out to greet me. The reason's soon clear – he doesn't want to be having this conversation where his guests might overhear.

'A sudden death?'

'Yes,' says Mackintosh, as I flip my notebook open. 'One of my regulars.'

He has a look that says he isn't entirely present, and he seems genuinely sad.

'Who discovered the body?'

'I did.'

'Anyone else with you at the time?'

'No.'

'What made you check on her?'

'She didn't come down for breakfast. She never misses it.'

'And last night?'

'She seemed fine. I welcomed her, saw her in the lounge once or twice and then she went off to bed. Now this.'

He looks down at his brown brogues and nudges a small pile of gravel away with his foot.

'Aye well. We'd best be seeing her then,' I say.

Mackintosh speaks in hushed tones as he leads the way. He treads more lightly than I'd expect for a man of his size.

'I'll need to go first,' I say. 'Procedure.'

He nods, and then slows, a few steps short of a white-glossed bedroom door. He twitches his head towards it and stands aside.

It's a cold house, Balmore. Like a lot of the old shooting lodges, it's granite built — which seems to seal the cold in rather than keep it out. Even so, there's a fine chill in this room.

She's dead, no doubt about it. I look around. No obvious disturbance, drawers neatly shut, window perfectly sealed, no indication of substance abuse or suicide. I finish the routine, then step back out into the hallway. Mackintosh's eyes are saying: please, please get this over with as quickly as possible.

'It looks OK, right enough,' I say, 'but we'll need CID along just to be sure there's nothing more to it. And you'll be wanting Dr Simpson to certify death and arrange for the body to be moved. Now, I'll just take a few details and gather her personal effects for the next of kin to collect.'

Mackintosh nods, then takes my elbow and steers me down the passage. I sense that he has something else to say.

As we reach the top of the stairs he lowers his voice. 'Now Lachlan, there is — um — a wee thing you'll need to know...'

The eyes have stories to tell, even in the glassy stare of death. Within three to four hours they begin to cloud as a thin film develops over them. As the pressure from the fluid behind them drops, the eyeballs themselves become softer, and the degree to which this has occurred can be used as a measure of the time elapsed since death.

This woman's eyes tell me she has been dead at least 12 hours, possibly more.

I wonder what shade they were. There's a slender rim of iris around the dilated pupil, but the colour is now indistinct through the clouding. Were hers green? I've never much liked green eyes on women. Still, the small creases tell me they were made for smiling and happiness. Pleasure even. She was attractive, there's no question of that. Probably in her mid-fifties, but looked younger.

The messaging service contacted me about the death at Balmore House. My first reaction – quite irrational – was fear that it might have been Mackintosh, the owner, who I like to think has become somewhat of a friend over the years.

'Who is it?' I asked.

'A guest.'

I felt a moment of guilty relief at the death of this stranger. Then guilty pleasure at the chance to escape the surgery and the daily drudgery of warts, colds and sexually transmitted diseases.

Now, not more than an hour later, I'm staring down at her lifeless form. I touch her hand and feel the coldness, then check for a pulse. Already she's become an empty shell. Yesterday a living, breathing being, no doubt with friends and family that cared for and loved her. And now this. It always ends the same way.

I look at her eyes once more and wonder what other stories they might have had to tell. Then I close the eyelids and pull up the sheet to cover her. Teal. That's what comes to me as I leave the room. Her eyes would have been teal.

PHILIP

When will my breath go back to normal? I feel like I've been up here on the roof for ages. I wonder if anyone saw me? But no one else ever seems to come here. Well, they're missing out — you can find out a lot about what's going on from up here. People think they're on their own outside, but they don't realise how much a watcher can see — and hear — from the roof. Most people don't notice a lot of things, actually.

It feels heavy in my hand — should I really have taken it? But there's something pretty... I was going to say 'cool' but that's not really it — about having a dead person's phone. And there it was, asking to be picked up, I couldn't have just left it there.

That was kind of weird, actually. Touching a dead person. Half of me feels a bit sick. But when I overheard Mr Mackintosh talking about her to that witch Janet — I'm sure she pokes around in my stuff when she's cleaning my room — I just had to go and see. I mean, when you find out someone's dead, in the room along the corridor, it's like, well, you've got to look, haven't you?

So I hung around until the corridor was empty and slipped into the bathroom opposite. The door to her room was slightly open and I could see someone moving around. Then he came out — the doctor I guessed — and went downstairs.

Now was the moment. I was a bit scared but then I thought — what would everyone at school say if they knew I'd had the chance but not taken it? I turned the handle really slowly and opened the door. I went in, and stopped just inside, leaving it a little bit open. I didn't like the idea of being shut inside with a dead person.

I could see a shape in the bed. For some reason I'd imagined she must've died in the loo. So she didn't. Unless that wasn't her. But it must be — though someone had pulled the sheet up over her head.

I went over to the bed on tiptoes. Somehow I couldn't quite walk properly in there. I reached out a hand, making sure I only touched the very edge of the sheet, and lifted it up a bit. I was scared now. What would she look like?

Actually it was a bit boring. She just looked asleep. No knives or blood or anything. There wasn't much to tell in that. Although I could've made something up, I suppose. Then I noticed the phone – peeping out between the leg of the bed and the skirting board. It must've fallen off the bedside table. Or perhaps... perhaps she'd been holding it at the moment she died and dropped it. I felt suddenly all shivery. I had to have it. It pulled me – my hand reached out and I shoved it in my pocket.

I was about to leave, and then I thought – what if I could tell them all I'd actually touched a body? So I turned back to the bed, pulled the sheet back again and reached out and poked her cheek really gently with my finger.

And then I really didn't want to be in there any more. It was weird touching her cheek. I mean, who touches adults' cheeks? Hers was clammy and the mark my finger made didn't come straight out again.

I put the sheet back, crept out of the room and shut the door really quietly. As soon I was out I ran. Right to the other end of the corridor, up the winding staircase and out onto the roof.

And here I am. I'm calming down now. That horrible tingly sweaty feeling is going. But I'm not sure I want this phone after all. The police are going to start asking questions, aren't they? They're going to want it. And maybe someone did see me after all. Maybe they'll say I nicked it – and then I'll be in huge trouble with Mum and Dad – I'm already on my last warning. And I didn't really nick it – it's only a borrow. But I really don't want to go back though. I don't want to see her again.

I know, I'll give it to him when he gets here.

I am thinking of adding a new line to our terms and conditions: 'Please note that if you are planning to die on your visit to Scotland, try to avoid Saturday and Sunday.' Getting anything done here at the weekend is almost impossible, let alone removing a body from a house full of paying guests.

Somehow we manage it. Old bachelor Simpson turns up and pokes about. How he can be both such a good doctor and such a curmudgeon is utterly beyond me. PC Lachlan does his best. He even persuades our fat, lazy bigot of an undertaker John Cattanach that a corpse can't be left in a hotel bedroom overnight.

I have a slightly tricky conversation with Lachlan. Years of dealing with small town misdemeanours have slowed his brain down to match the ponderous bounce of his walk. I try to explain the delicacy of the situation but that broad freckled Highland mug just stares blankly back at me.

'Not her real name,' he repeats, glancing down at the register. He writes each word in his notebook like a child learning how to read. 'Now, why would that be?'

'That isn't really my business,' I tell him, trying to remain patient and aware that we are being watched by two of the TV people who are here up from London scouting for suitably 'Highland' locations for yet another remake of *Kidnapped*.

'She's a regular visitor and comes to stay with an old friend of mine.' I pause. 'They aren't married.'

Lachlan looks up at me and blinks. 'You mean they've children out of wedlock? You said the family would need to be informed?'

'No, her children aren't his children.' It's as though I've asked him to solve a particularly difficult crossword clue. I can see cogs turning slowly.

'She's divorced then?' I really don't have time for this, and now young Philip is gawping at us. I really wish his parents would keep him under some measure of control.

'No, Lachlan. She and my friend have been having an affair for years. They come here for the same weekend in March, without fail. They book under the names Miranda and Bill Tempest. Don't ask me why.

Her marriage is an unhappy one. That's all I know. I run a shooting lodge and guesthouse, not a marriage guidance service. It's not my place to judge, nor, I would remind you, is it yours.'

That shuts him up. He closes his notebook, smiles in a 'say no more' kind of way and asks if he can use the house phone.

Day 2

SUNDAY

RICHARD

The bell rings and a uniformed cliché stands there on the doorstep, a grim-faced policeman with the dull note of death in his voice. 'Are you Mr Richard White? Is your mother Iris White?'

When it's yourself, you never know how you're going to take it. Boot on the other foot. Hearing things through the other end of the stethoscope. Just because doctors are used to giving news of death doesn't mean they know how to receive it. Doesn't mean I know.

So. Mum's dead. My mind processes that somehow. This ridiculously young bobby standing in my hallway tells me the news. I'm not old but he somehow manages to be younger than me and doing a job that takes a bit of experience. Seems I'm always the elder one.

So the elder brother's responsibility kicks in. Do I offer him a cup of tea? Julia, would you mind? She looks solicitous so, of course, she offers tea. Tea and solicitude. Two sugars for the young bobby – it will make it easier for him as he sits uncomfortably at our kitchen table.

'We need you to identify the body, sir,' he suggests.

Where is it? Where did you say she died? Died. It's just a word. Slips in and out of mouths as easily as taking a pill. Just a word but now a word that applies to my mother. When I'd always applied other words to her, in other tenses. She dances. She sings. She laughs. She loves me. She'll be coming over later.

But not any more.

And I just can't understand. Why die in such a place? Not here in north London. Not in her own home, in her own bed, but in some strange house and some strange bed in the furthest, coldest, bleakest part of the country.

Mum, *you* never let me down before. Dad – yes, he did, all the time. I'd expect it of him but not you. Why, Mum? Why? I could have done without this.

And why does death come knocking on my front door on a late afternoon of an early spring day that feels like winter? I'm already low and feeling now I can only go lower. Inside and outside it's getting dark, and I need to be busy, to do something. Where is Balmore House?

How do I get there?

Julia closes the door on the policeman. I wince. As if she's shutting Mum outside, and I'm not sure what's left inside.

1. Solomon

a) called, left message with brief news, tried to be sensitive but 'I've got very bad news. About Iris. In a hotel in the Scottish Highlands. I'm sorry but please call me' was the best I could do... Will await call.

b) emailed him to give me a call.

c) texted to let him know I'd emailed.

d) not sure if any of this got through – try again tomorrow.

2. Robin

a) called, spoke to him, as expected a uniquely Robin combination of upset and stoned, more the latter I suspect. He is a sweetie though, hope he'll join Richard in Scotland.

b) called again later just to make sure he had been listening.

3. Rebecca

a) sat with her and explained calmly what the policeman had said. This will be most difficult for her. Do not think it wise for her to go on the trip (*see note re Richard below*).

b) went to her room later that night, the sweetheart needs cuddles. Always did.

4. Richard

a) unsurprisingly stoic, remarkably practical. No tears. Later perhaps. Thought he'd 'disappear' again, as with Archie's birth. Instead, he's organising the trip to the Highlands!

b) told him that Rebecca should not go: too young, too teenage. Richard reluctant, Rebecca naturally curious and insistent. So off they go.

c) we shared a bottle of wine. We didn't talk. It was... nice.

5. The kids

a) too young to understand, but we did our best – didn't mention the 'd' word, said Grandma had gone to sleep forever... Now it sounds like we were talking about a dog.

b) tucked up and sound asleep. Adorable.

6. Iris

a) why Scotland?

b) will miss you. Greatly.

ROBIN

Adie exhales a jet stream of blue-grey smoke and hands me the pipe. About fucking time. Just as I'm fixing to take a draw the phone rings; I roll across the sofa and pick up. Since Drew got sent down last month I've had feelers out for a new contact and I somehow felt sure this would be the call to say, yes, my man is holding and it's good and he wants – nay, demands – you buy his gear *right now*. Instead I hear a woman's voice, familiar but not in an everyday way.

'Hello Robin? Oh I'm so glad I've caught you. This is Julia, you know, Richard's wife.'

Oh God, probably the last person I want to speak to. All the time I've known her she's dropped not-so-subtle hints about her wild years as a teenage party girl (usually accompanied by a conspiratorial giggle and those air quote gestures I really hate). I've never had the heart to tell her that screwing half of Kent doesn't make us soulmates.

I take a huge hit and hold it down – we could be talking for hours and I'm not delaying my gratification for anyone. Plus Adie will want the pipe back in a mo and I want my share. But even as my brain reels from the tsunami of THC I'm wondering why Julia is calling. She's never been in touch before. I sense trouble.

'Mmm, yeah, hello Julia, it's... er, Robin here.' Fuck, why did I say that? She knows who you are, you idiot, *she* called *you*.

Brief silence, in which I imagine Julia generously trying to interpret my garbled response in any way other than the obvious.

'Well, the thing is, it's... well Robin, I've some terrible news. I'm afraid your mum has died suddenly. In Scotland. I'm so sorry.'

It's funny what you focus on in Life's Big Moments. I remember when Hannah told me she was pregnant all I could think about was a bit of fluff on the carpet in front of us, until I ended up vacuuming while she sobbed and stormed out. I wonder what happened to her? Now all I could think was, 'Scotland? What was she doing up there?' I dimly recall conferences in the past but I'd no idea she was still in demand north of the border.

'Oh my God. That's... that's terrible. Just... *terrible*.' Nice one Robin, exactly the sort of thing you're supposed to say. But if I'm honest I feel...

well, nothing. Our relationship had been strained since before I was a teenager and we'd hardly spoken for years. Still, that doesn't mean I wanted her dead. Not like that Russian bloke Mark and I scored off last week in Kennington; now he really deserves to die, in fact...

'...so obviously there are arrangements to make and things we need to do as a family to bring her home.' We? Family? Ironic, considering I'm running in the opposite direction. Still, just agree and hope she goes away.

'Yes, yes... obviously. Obviously!'

Another perplexed silence. 'Are you... all right Robin? You don't sound... well.'

'No I'm, er, fine, yeah fine, Julia, under the... circumstances. It's just such a shock. I... I can't think clearly.' That last sentence, at least, is true. I'm really starting to lose it here.

This only seems to encourage my sister-in-law. 'Oh I'm not surprised, Richard is in pieces − *I bet he fucking is, loves a bit of drama, my bro* − and you'll have your own grieving to do − *will I? Don't be too sure* − but we were wondering − *uh-oh, here we go* − if you could go up to Scotland with him the day after tomorrow? He doesn't want to just take Rebecca − *Child of Doom is coming along? No wonder Rich doesn't want to go alone, Our Sister of the Perpetual Scowl isn't anyone's ideal travelling companion* − and he felt sure you'd want to play your part.'

Which just shows how wrong you can be. Let Mr Perfect go. It'll give him a great opportunity to worry, furrow his brows and wipe away the occasional noble tear. And he is a doctor, used to death and bodies and stuff; what use would I be? The only corpse I've ever seen was that poor girl in the New Cross squat, and that gave me nightmares for a month. But never mind that right now, I'm absolutely fucking fucked. I'm going to have to lie down before I fall down. I'll deal with this later, really I will...

'The two of them will be flying to Inverness from Luton Airport at 11.10 on Tuesday morning, so shall I tell him you'll meet him at the easyJet information desk at say 8.30? You can get some breakfast and talk. Robin? Robin, are you there...?'

REBECCA

OMG mum's dead. She's dead. A HEART ATTACK. Can u believe that? Fuck. I thought only men got heart attacks. I mean she drank HERBAL TEA. So like I could die of a heart attack one day. That's fucked.

iMessage, 17 Mar 2013 17:21

Wish i could see you and talk. You're the only one who understands. Ive got no one else to talk to. No one. I dont know whats gonna happen now. It'll just be me and dad. Unless he decides to pack me off to Dishwater and Bossypants.

iMessage, 17 Mar 2013 17:24

Oh no silly me keep forgetting!!! But we'll have to wait a bit longer. Wish i could talk to you. Get in touch when u can. Reb

iMessage, 17 Mar 2013 17:25

IRIS

When you three were babes-in-arms I whispered the same promises onto the tops of your heads over and over again. And then I told them to your cheeks and I spoke them into your curling hands and feet. And then I repeated them to you every night before you went to sleep.

Do you remember? 'Night night, sleep tight, don't let the bed bugs bite.' (Except you, Richard, you liked me to call them the 'bed buds', insisted on it, and how could I not agree?) And then I said, 'I love you forever and ever and I will be with you forever and ever because that's what I'm here for.'

As you grew older the words got faster, pummelled from my lips at juggernaut speed as you pretended you were too old to be tucked in. But still I whispered them, like a prayer, pressed close against your hair so you could feel the weight of them. I meant every word.

Before Rebecca started school, the four of us would spend lazy summer evenings in the garden while Solomon strutted around his office. We'd gather herbs, puff on dandelion clocks, name silly plants (*foxsocks, delias, rosies*). I'd spin her around my body six times.

How I wish we had stayed like that in perpetual motion. For if time slowed down, if the watches stopped, like the pearl moon face on my wrist at five to nine on Friday evening, I would have time to say:

You do not know how much you mean to me. I have saved this book for you, read it. Water that plant, rescue that bee, switch off the radio, listen, look at the beauty around you. Be gentle and kind, do dare and never presume, squeeze your sadness into a ball and roll it towards me.

Day 3

MONDAY

ROBIN

BANG BANG BANG BANG. Fuck, *definitely* the cops. No one else knocks like that before CBeebies comes on air.

In the hours after Julia's call Adie and I worked through a bale of weed before I ventured out to buy a large bottle of Frosty Jack cider from our local kebab shop (22 units for £5.75, obligingly wrapped like a large doner to avoid awkward questions from Lambeth Council's licensing department). Suitably stoked I lay there until the early hours, failing to feel any real distress. While I was growing up all I wanted was Mother's approval, but instead she was always busy, always away. It was no fun taking second place to one of her precious plants. Now things are different. Now it's my turn not to care.

I stumble downstairs into the hall and look through the spyhole. Two plainclothes and four – count 'em – uniform. Must be serious for this show of strength. As I open the door a blast of cold air shoots up my dressing gown causing me to flinch before our visitors. Behind them Brixton Road is coming to life, with passengers on the first bus of the day suddenly interested in our little sideshow. It's something to look at I suppose.

Blinking in the grey light I recognise a couple of faces. 'DC Scrooby. And is that Sergeant Creake I see? To what do I owe...'

'Morning, Robin. Is Willis here?'

Ah, that would explain it. Mark Willis, our occasional flatmate, is also an occasional bad boy. Rather more than occasional actually.

'Haven't seen him for a week, Detective. No idea where he is. I've been busy. Minicabbing. Painting and decorating. Working on the novel.' All true. Except the last bit.

'Of course. The novel. Mind if we look around?' And in they come, skidding on the scree of fried chicken flyers and stumbling up the stairs to the first floor flat. What choice did I have? Avoid antagonising the Met, that's my rule. It might save me a good hiding in the back of a van one day.

I follow the two detectives into the kitchen while the uniforms go from room to room. God knows what Adie will think if he regains consciousness.

'So what's Mark been up to this time?'

'Demanding money with menaces. Again.' He clocks last night's overflowing ashtray and its incriminating contents but clearly couldn't give a toss.

'No friend of mine, Mr Scrooby, he just crashes here when he feels like it. We can't stop him, really.'

'I'm sure. Well, if you happen to see him let him know we called. Of course — *theatrical pause* — it might be better for you if you *didn't* see him.'

'Oh? And why's that?' Scrooby lobbed his informational IED into the conversation knowing I'd have to ask. It doesn't sound good.

'It seems Mr Willis was in The Black Bear last night claiming you're responsible for our current interest in him. As a result he's threatening "vile retribution". His exact words apparently. You might want to consider that a warning.'

Five minutes later I'm escorting our visitors to the front door while desperately trying to remember where I left Julia's number. Anything is preferable to Mad Mark and his vile retribution. I've seen what he can do with the contents of the average cutlery drawer, a memory that makes a few days away from south London seem an incredibly attractive proposition.

So get this, mum died in Scotland. Dunno what she was doing there. She never goes to Scotland. Sure she was going to Cornwall. Goes there lots. Went. Fuck. Or was it Devon? Hope they dont wanna drag me along. It's horrible and everything, but SCOTLAND… If I can get them out of my hair maybe I can even meet you.

iMessage, 18 Mar 2013 11:47

So get this, Dishwater wants to leave me at home with Bossypants. No fucking way! I'm supposed to rot in darkest suburbia and suffer death by vapid small talk while he gets to swan off to Scotland and take care of everything about mum. I should be protected or some such paternalistic crap. She's my mum too. Ive got the same rights. Hes my brother not my dad. No way I'm not going. No way.

iMessage, 18 Mar 2013 16:17

Read that Baudelaire u talked about. SO TRUE – no one gets what its like to be a poet. Fave line: Would whole knots of vipers were my spawn, rather than to have fed this derisive object! Said it ALL for me. Thx Heathcliffe you really understand – you're more me than I am myself! Tell more about Paris. What will we see? What poetry will you read me?

iMessage, 18 Mar 2013 18:39

I'm motionless in front of my laptop. The only thing that's moving is the ancient ceiling fan, which pretends to stir the air in the coffee bar of my hotel. If I wasn't so sentimental, and more to the point, broke, I could book in to somewhere modern and air-conditioned. My motionlessness could easily have been caused by humid torpor, which is often the case in Cuba, but this time it's shock. Sheer dumb shock, the clichéd reaction to the unexpected loss of a loved one. But it turns out that it's what happens.

I look down at my mobile phone. Julia had left a garbled message that I didn't understand, other than the alarm in her voice, but before I could ring her back, she had rung again.

'Solomon, it's Julia.' I was astonished, and that must have been obvious.

'Yes, I know, you can't have been expecting it. Solomon...' And it was her saying my name again, and the catch in her voice, that gave me the instant knowledge.

'Iris? Oh my God. Iris.'

'I'm so sorry. I'm truly sorry.' I could hear the gratitude in her voice that she didn't have to say it.

'What? How? When?'

'It looks like a heart attack, but we don't know for certain yet. There will be a post mortem. Solomon...' There was another pause in her voice, which served to put me on notice. What could be worse than that my wife was dead? 'There's also a where to this news.'

'Where? So, where? Where was she?'

'On a remote estate in the Highlands of Scotland.'

'What?' My brain was scrambled. 'Why?'

'Um, we were all hoping you might know.'

I was on the point of saying that I thought she was in Paris, but stopped myself. I was being put in the position of covering the tracks for my wife, after she'd managed to get herself caught red-handed in her own death.

'Er, Julia. Her field trips took her to all sorts of unlikely places. There's plenty to study up there.'

'Of course.' A silence opened between us. I must not have sounded convincing, but Julia's discretion was absolute. I had my first thought about Richard.

'So, Richard. He must be on his way presumably? Or he would be calling?'

'Oh, Richard is just...' She stopped herself again. 'Yes, exactly.' So he wasn't. What a complete shit my eldest son is. Even at a moment like this, he couldn't bring himself to talk to me. This feels like the final straw. I'm not sure of what, but of something.

The call with Julia tailed off into her solicitous questions about how I was, then into what a wonderful woman Iris was, and then came some logistical talk about getting back, and I already can't remember how it ended. The bartender came straight over, reading the signs of something momentous passing across my face. I mumbled something at him which he didn't comprehend, but, notwithstanding it was only mid-morning, he brought a large rum, indicating it was on the house. I've yet to touch it.

My laptop has gone to sleep, its basalt screen acting as a dim mirror. I look terrible. I'm no oil painting, unless you happen to have a bit of a thing for doughy, bald men the wrong side of fifty-five. And not many people do, including Iris. She certainly doesn't. Well, didn't. Correcting myself to think of her in the past tense is the first realisation. Disastrous news still calls for good grammar.

I may not have moved, but I have thought a lot these last thirty minutes. And felt even more. Emotions and memories mixing together all the primary colours of pain in front of my eyes; no kind of mental quality control over my brain. No energy to be ashamed, I'm appalled at the audit of what's been going on, but what the fuck?

There's logistical fatigue: I've got the pure horror ahead of negotiating airline bureaucracy to fly home.

There's misplaced professional pride: the fantasy of ignoring the circumstance and giving a great conference speech. 'I can't believe you managed to deliver that profound critique of Western capitalism in the twentieth century under those circumstances. Such force of passion.

And your poor wife.' 'Oh, not at all. I think dedicating it to her helped me to find the inner strength. And she'd have wanted me to stay on and deliver it. It would have been her wish.' Like she would have given a flying fuck either way.

There's fury with Richard: fancy delegating this job to the dutiful and caring wife that he doesn't deserve. Priggish, uptight, self-serving and humourless. And don't get me started on his bad points. Actually, I quite like that, and if I hadn't been so angry with him I might have smiled. As it is, the moment I think of him, I ring him on impulse. Julia answers but I insist on speaking to my son. At the end of a short, one-sided conversation I wish I hadn't.

My hand briefly flutters in the direction of the rum, but stalls as the list goes on. There's wildly unacceptable selfishness: the fleeting, inadmissible concern (repulsive even to me) that the funeral might coincide with West Ham's away fixture with Newcastle, and my annual weekend with Alan, my oldest friend and just about the only person in the world I don't have to justify myself to. I told Julia to pass a message on to Richard to take care of things until I can get back, but in fact I'll have to try and stay as close to the arrangements as possible. It's a racing certainty that Richard will colonise the organisation of our family mourning.

RICHARD

I could have been a better son. The regrets come flooding in now that Mum's no longer here, now that I can't say anything to her. I wish I'd said more I wish I'd said goodbye properly I wish she'd said goodbye to me.

There are always these regrets, the what-ifs. But then the banalities of life take over. Or perhaps it's the banalities of death. Nothing, no one, is more banal than brother Robin. I don't get I really don't get what goes on inside his head. But there doesn't seem to be much there. I listen as Julia breaks the news to him – for a second time.

'Robin,' Julia says, 'it's Mum. She's gone.'

'Gone where?' he asks in a voice from far far away.

'Gone. Passed away.' There's still only silence. 'She died, Robin.'

We don't talk much. Robin can't find the words for me. We didn't talk much, ever. The truth is we don't have much in common. He's younger by five years and that was always too much to be close. He's been happy to waste his life away on drugs and drink and sheer, well, irresponsibility, if I'm being kind to him. But who cares? Don't think he does. Not sure Dad does either. It was only Mum could stand him.

I spoke to Dad just now, on a crackly phone line from Cuba. What a time to be away, leaving me with all this. I wouldn't have minded if the policeman had told me *it's your dad, he's dead*. But there he is thousands of miles away, sucking up to Castro's minions and puffing on a cigar to express solidarity. While I'm here with a dead mum in Scotland, a body to identify, a flight to arrange and two younger siblings to herd into line. Dad's last words to me on the phone: 'Make things right for your mum, see to it, Richard.'

I could scream. *Shall I?* No, stay calm, that's your job, doctor.

So I stick to the practical details. There's a flight to Inverness tomorrow morning, then a cab ride of thirty miles. That's what the man at the hotel says. Is Robin coming? He says he is, but who knows? I'm getting him a ticket, I couldn't do anything else. He'd only make a scene at the airport if I try to keep him away. But will he even show up?

Then there's Rebecca. Oh God, there's Rebecca. I really really don't want her to come. But she insists as only a spoilt fifteen-year-old can.

The plain fact is, that's another thing I got landed on me. Mum's away at one conference, Paris she told me, and Dad's at another in Cuba. 'So would you mind, Richard, you and Julia, could Rebecca stay with you while we're away?'

What could I do? I could have said No, I could have been a bad son, I could have been a bad brother. But that's not my way.

Rebecca doesn't make it any easier. All right, I know it's hard for her. But it's harder for me, it really is. I'm the one who has to do the organising, I have to think for the others. Rebecca can play act at grief while I hold things together.

That's the way it is. So here I am at the computer in my study. Three tickets to Inverness. easyJet. One step up from Ryanair at least. Packing a bag with enough for a couple of days. Checking my doctor's bag, that comes with me everywhere, checking I've got the basics, instruments and everyday emergency drugs. And the handwritten scrap of paper, it still travels everywhere in the bag with me, 'Tread softly because you tread on my dreams.'

W.B. Yeats. Given to me by Lucy half my life ago, just teenagers then, just a teenage crush stored away, take when needed. And now right now feeling like a teenager still.

I smile sadly at Julia as she pokes her head round the door, treading on eggshells so as not to upset me. Not the girl of my dreams, but she's a good wife and I have two children and no regrets.

1. Solomon

a) we spoke. Solomon shocked, not least that I called, not Richard.

b) realised afterwards that he hadn't understood my message. Poor Solomon — will need to be in London to support him when he gets back as Richard will be in Scotland.

c) he rang again and demanded to speak to Richard — handed over phone and left room.

2. Robin

a) is he going to Scotland or not? Still don't know. Perhaps it's a little unfair on Richard. But then I 'get' Robin. I spent my youth screwing half of Kent. Richard is entirely different.

3. Rebecca

a) in her own world. A bit worried about her. Insists on going to Scotland. Wish she wouldn't.

4. Richard

a) stoic as ever. He's never been good at expressing his feelings. I used to admire that in him. But, now I'm a mother, I think I'd want some visible grief from my children if I died...

b) have packed his bags and contacted his practice to arrange locum.

c) insists on making own travel arrangements. Wish he'd let me help more.

6. Iris

a) need to plan the funeral. She told me once she wanted a Christian funeral. She liked the rituals. And lots of flowers, definitely. Richard must decide. Or Solomon. But I think she'd have wanted the local firm to handle it.

b) Iris in hospital morgue. In the Highlands.

c) I am struggling to understand how such an organised woman could have ended up in such a random place.

You won't believe this. I posted on FB about mum and 17 people LIKED it. That's more likes than some of my photos get. Or ANY of my poems. This is so screwed.

iMessage, 18 Mar 2013 21:21

Rebecca White Attention Facebook 'friends'. I post that my mum died and 17 people like it. What the hell's WRONG with you people? I'm going through hell and you LIKE it? You try losing someone close – see how you LIKE that.
Posted at 21:29pm

Like · Share · Comment

Rebecca White @rebwhite   3m
How do you delete a Facebook post?

SOLOMON

There's a power surge in the bar. The lights strengthen and the fan finds a new lease of life. I stare at it, getting dizzy trying to follow one of the blades. I feel disorientated: Iris has been in the centre of my life for more than half my time on this planet. What does it mean to not have her there any longer? I have no idea what its significance is. The thought of it makes me nauseous, as if on a theme park ride. All bearings lost, connection to the rootedness of earth gone.

There are what ifs: principally what if I'd chosen Stella when it was clear she was interested? How different would my life have been? There's an outrageous, guilty suspicion that any children we'd have had would have been more of a consolation (how could they not have been?). And thinking about Stella makes me realise that, unlike Richard's evasion, there are going to be some phone calls I will have to make, however difficult they'll be. She'll be first; I want her to hear it from me.

There's doubt: the whole Robin question, which I always try to bury, but which bubbles up and refuses to go away. I could feel this one rising to the surface unbidden, and tried to chase it away with even more unpalatable memories, but it came back anyway. In fact, I sincerely hope he is mine. There's honesty and an integrity of motivation with him that Richard knows nothing about. But Robin's straightforward. Dope – the friend that keeps on taking.

There's the jolt of fresh responsibility: having to manage Rebecca. She has always been Iris's province and I know I've been lazy around her. I was already tired of parenting when she came along. But seriously, how am I supposed to make sense of her, and help her through what's left of her minority? Hartley said that the past is a foreign country. Rubbish. It's the present that's alien territory. It's enough to make me break out like an Edwardian colonel. 'Funny chaps, girls. Knew one once. No idea what the deuce she was on about most of the time. Never got involved with the distaff side since.'

And then in and amongst and around all of this is Iris. A variety of women have walked into the bar over the past half hour, and all of them look like Iris. Like you.

Iris. I'm sure that missing you is going to hit me soon, but right here, right now, I'm stunned by the feeling of anger. I can feel it starting to pour out of me and onto the floor like a lake of poisoned blood. How dare you? How could you do this to us, to yourself, to me? I'm calling out to you in confusion, in the rawness of having heard that you're dead. Can you hear me? I'm here, amongst the familiar brilliance and smoky heat of my Havana, hearing of you dying in a wintry, remote Scottish lodge. How more separate could we be? And the bitter irony of hearing the news here, the place where we honeymooned; young and intoxicated by life and love and music and Havana spice.

Your death feels careless. Selfish, and self-inflicted. There is no acceptable reason for you to have died up there. No reason connected to us as a family. It's a death that's all about you and a life that we have no part in. You told me that you were going to be in Paris for your spring conference, just like me out here. Your sense of direction was never that good, but even you should have worked out by Durham at the latest that you were going the wrong way. So what were you doing up there? Of course, as has become our custom, I didn't quiz you about this conference. And for that latitude, you owed it to me, to all of us, not to screw up. But you have, haven't you? Massively. So now, we're all going to have to make sense of this, and I suspect what they have no idea about; that it's not a sense that any of us are going to like. It will leave us insensible.

And so I'm angry with you. I'm enraged. Not only that, but I still love you, and I think I may hate you for that. Or hate myself. I love you, despite all the fissures that have opened up between us over the years. I even think I may still be in love with you. I love you for your vivacity, strength, mothering, refusal to give up on your ancient Beetle, tolerance, intelligence, your lyrical way with words, the mole behind your left ear, your plants and bee hives, your spaghetti carbonara, and a million other things that are filling my head. It's taken your death to feel the depth, breadth and sheer quantity of things to love you for. Is this why they refer to the dead as 'the late Iris' or whoever? Because all the realisations are too late?

I'm tired. As I continue looking at the laptop, a few tears have irrigated these desiccated cheeks. I'm suddenly weary, and definitely wary. Wary of the future, and the isolation within my own family that I suspect she shielded me from more than I know. So, to circle back once more, how dare she?

    And how dare I have let her go?

Day 4

TUESDAY

Another morning, another drive to the surgery. There's been an outbreak of verrucas. The local children dodge the cold footbath at the swimming pool and spread their infections to all and sundry. Little sewer rats.

I fire up the Range Rover's old diesel engine. It rumbles like someone trying to clear his throat and eventually splutters into life. The car's twenty years old, one of the few things in my world that I can trust absolutely. The Balmore woman's post-mortem has come back clean. All that remains now is to put the family in touch with Cattanach's and get the paperwork over to Lachlan.

But I can't get her eyes out of my head, clouded though they were. As clouded as her identity. She registered as Miranda Tempest, yet her real name was Iris White. Hardly the action of an honest woman. Not that I know much about honest women. My own few – they hardly merit the description of relationships – dalliances let's say, they all ended badly.

Iris. What I do know is that the iris is nakedly visible muscle, a poly-chrome halo of pigmentation around the pupil. It's also one of the most beautiful manifestations of the life force itself. And an oddly vital name for a corpse, now that I come to think of it.

Well, whatever her nature, or her name for that matter, she certainly didn't expect to die in a bed in the Scottish Highlands. She was from London somewhere, and Mackintosh implied that she had been on some sort of tryst.

Maybe her eyes were green after all. Iris Green...

RICHARD

At least I'm not sat next to Robin or Rebecca. Plane check-ins these days seem to delight in scattering you around, even if you'd wanted to sit together. I didn't. I wanted a break. Getting Rebecca up on time, meeting Robin at the airport, talking grumpily over a cup of coffee, making sure Rebecca was still tagging along... enough.

So I got a window seat, a chance to gaze out at blue sky above the clouds. A chance to think. A chance to work out why this happened, and what to do next. I could have been a pilot and been happy. I could have enjoyed living above the clouds.

Medically there's nothing to wonder at, unless you're still surprised at nitroglycerin to treat angina. It's normal, it won't explode, I tell my patients. They smile. I'd known about Mum's heart. If she'd been my patient, I'd have given her the same prescription. She looked after herself but with hearts you never know, they can break anytime, I've seen it happen with lots of patients. It can happen just like that.

No, it's not the dying that puzzles me. It's everything else. Why am I now flying to Scotland? Because a few days ago she'd flown to Scotland. And why was that? Because she was attending the annual botanical conference in Paris. The answers have a big gap between them.

I think of Mum and I think of flowers. They were her life. Plants and flowers. Not in a florist kind of way, or as a gardener, or even as a pure academic. But she believed that plants could save us all, and would save us all, if we just understood them better. She wrote papers on it, she got paid by pharmaceutical companies, she gave talks at symposia. And people listened, from all around the world.

I loved her for that. I wish I could have done as much with my life. But my knowledge is strictly general, nothing as specialised as the medicinal properties of an alpine saxifrage. A general practitioner not a spotter of mountain Erica. Not that I ever knew what her special areas of knowledge really were. There's a lot about Mum that I didn't know.

I remember the only time I'd been to Scotland before. We had a cottage for a week near Loch Ness. The idea had been a quiet time away from it all. I think I was six or seven, but I can't remember Robin being there, even as a baby presence. I can't remember my dad either – perhaps he stayed at home. But there were plants on the hills and in the valleys and by the banks of rivers. Mum told me their names and I got to identify them. We started with *Calluna* and she made it sound the most beautiful word I'd heard. She told me it means cleansing, and I liked that, a plant with a purpose, not just decorative. Even *Calluna vulgaris* made the purpose sound less than common.

It was in countryside like that below, looking down as the plane banks. There's a greenness in the landscape but it's tinged with shades of brown, it's not the lush green of English grass. There's snow on the hilltops too, rivers of white flowing down the cracks through the rocks. Like icy lava. It's supposed to be spring but the land looks deep-frozen.

That holiday, others like it in other places, were precious because of Mum. Time spent with her was time well spent. She made life burst into life. She loved books so we all loved books. We adopted her passions even when we didn't understand them. She had a curiosity about things, and she passed it on. Foxglove in our garden is *digitalis*, it's good for hearts. I got interested in medicine. But it got twisted, away from where I wanted it to be, twisted into a GP. I could have been an academic, researching my own field of interest. Except I never discovered a field to properly be interested in.

The plane bumps onto the tarmac runway. Back to earth with a bump. Things to do: go to the baggage carousel, collect my bag; round up Robin and Rebecca; find a taxi to take us to Balmore; call the hotel from the taxi, confirm we'll stay at least one night, more if needed; find out about identifying Mum's body.

I'd rather not. I'd rather be somewhere else. But there's no escape. Robin and Rebecca follow behind me like stalkers.

REBECCA

Dearest H, just landed in Scotland. Inverness. Raining. God what a hole. Havent seen the monster yet. Robin came with us, not seen him for yonks. Missed him so much – he's the only one who gets me. In the fam I mean.

Robin's a free spirit. Seemed kinda nervy when we met up at the airport. Think hes really upset. Hoped to talk about stuff but he sprinted to the loo soon as the seatbelt sign went off and spent half the flight there. Think he was crying cos he looked all red eyed when he got back. Then he just slept for the rest of the flight. Had to endure a Dishwater diatribe on my schoolwork schedule when we landed.

iMessage, 19 Mar 2013 13:14

Our taxi passes through a village. Every house seems covered in the same beige-grey pebbledash I saw in such abundance on our journey from Inverness. It's as though the entire nation rose up as one and declared, 'Yes! We shall make our homes as mean and ugly as possible! What d'you think of *that*, yer soft English shite?'

On the edge of town I notice a pub called The Claymore that looks a good place to score; Staffie-toting scum in nylon leisurewear throng the entrance – always an encouraging sign. As we head further out I have to lean over Rebecca and crane my neck to see the top of the nearest mountain, before realising it's a molehill compared to the monstrous peaks ahead. I try to get a better look but Richard's head obscures much of the scenery. God, if I were thinning like that I'd do the decent thing and get a crop, not ignore it like bro seems to be doing – although for once I seem to be the winner in life's little lottery.

Ten minutes later we're pulling up outside the rather grand Balmore House. If the exterior is impressive, the large hallway, as glimpsed through the wide open front door, is a taxidermist's wet dream. All creatures great and small adorn the walls, glassy-eyed and distinctly dead. Would it be wrong to suggest adding Iris to the collection, saving ourselves the grief of getting her south? Just as I'm musing on the moral implications of having one's mother stuffed, a florid-looking man emerges, carried along by a pack of boisterous terriers.

'Good afternoon, and welcome, welcome to Scotland! I'm David, David Mackintosh, host here at Balmore.' He's on autopilot, coming on strong with the bonhomie before suddenly remembering who we are and why we're here. He continues in a far more solemn tone.

'Now, you must be Richard? And this is Robin and, er, Rebecca? There's certainly a strong resemblance.'

'To our dead mother? Sweet of you to notice.' Rebecca glowers at David, even more moody than before we arrived – and she was pretty moody then. Come on Becs, he didn't deserve that.

We're all wondering what to say when a glum-looking policeman appears. My first thought was that DC Scrooby-do must have warned the local plod I'm trouble. But no, one look at this fellow and I realise there's no need to flush my stash. Steady, dependable and slightly dim – that's my on-the-spot assessment. As far as he knows I'm just a grieving child come to collect my poor dead mum.

'This is PC Lachlan who will oversee the identification at the morgue,' our host informs us.

'We should go there directly,' intones the gloomy lawman. 'Which one of you will be performing the sad duty?'

Let's see. Should it be the doctor well versed in the ways of life and death, or the brilliant but as yet undiscovered man of letters who gets squeamish at the sight of a poorly pigeon? On balance I think the former. Clearly Richard feels the same way as he gamely volunteers.

The two of them head for Lachlan's car. Oh to be a fly on the dashboard and experience the repartee and recherché wit that will surely enliven their grim task. Meanwhile it seems Rebecca and I will have to content ourselves with whatever comforts Balmore House can offer.

'A bad business. A very bad business,' says our host, shaking his head as he ushers us indoors. He leads us through the hallway and into a large and comfortable room complete with blazing fire and yet more dead heads on the walls. I'm not clear if he means bad for Mother, him or us. I'd say Iris has definitely come off worst.

'We'll get your bags up to your rooms in a moment. There's no hurry, dinner is at 8.30. Until then, well, given the circumstances I expect you're thirsty.'

He throws open the doors to what I took to be a medium sized wardrobe. Before me lies a veritable sea of whiskies begging to be explored.

'You know, David, I expect you're right.'

PHILIP

'The family's arriving today — they'll be here after lunch.' I overheard Mr Mackintosh saying it on the phone to someone while I was waiting for breakfast to start. It's useful being early for things. Gives you an excuse to be somewhere — no one can tell you off for being early.

Mum said, 'Don't go and bother the poor man when he gets here, Philip.' But then she said that last year, about bothering him, I mean, but he said he liked having someone to play Angry Birds with. He was quite good actually, but not as good as me. And anyway I needed to give him the phone. I really didn't want it any more.

I'm not sure who 'they' are — I thought it was just him. But maybe she's got brothers and sisters, and they're coming. Or maybe her mum's still alive.

Now it's after lunch and I'm waiting in my room — I told Mum and Dad I'm watching a film. But really I'm sitting by the window, looking out onto the drive so I won't miss him. I like having this room. It's like being on the roof — you can see what's going on without anyone seeing you.

Finally a taxi comes up and I think it must be him. But three strangers get out — one's a girl a bit older than me — so I know it's not her family.

But then Mr Mackintosh comes out to meet them with that policeman. I've got my window open a bit and I hear him say something about how sorry he is about their mother!

I suddenly want to laugh but I can't because they'll hear me and then there'll be trouble. They must have phoned the wrong people and now these people think their mum's died!

I wish I could be a fly on the wall at the morgue though. Imagine when they see her and it's not their mum!

CALLUM

'Wait here!' the old man says, shout-whispering, and slams the door. The back door of the van opens, closes. The trolley scrapes over the gravelled concrete, and I watch John Cattanach Funeral Director, legend in his own Highland mind, turn himself sideways to get through the door, into the hospital morgue. I don't move limb nor muscle. And why would I? 'Wait here!' he said, like I'm the one who has problems with not moving. Like I'd have any trouble with sitting here watching my breath make a skin on the windows, until the snow-specks and grey air could be fog, or just nothing – no hospital building, no ambulance.

A minute passes, two minutes. My breath wipes out the morgue part of the building, my stepfather in it. And that's when I see the plant, inside one of the windows. It looks like an orchid. I wait, breathing shallow so not to erase it, watching a nurse walk up from inside and fluff at the plant's stalk, at its blossoms, pretending to care for it. *Don't touch it*, I want to say to her. *Don't. That's delicate.*

My feet make no sound on the paving. When I get to the window, the nurse has already moved on. Only one patient, an old lady, lies in a bed, on oxygen. Hip operation, probably. I watch for a minute, seeing myself in the glass, blurry and doubled, my skin seeming pale, almost green, my eyes dark and bloodshot, my cheeks looking even more hollow than normal. I smile and would swear there are fangs.

The old lady's asleep. I reach in and turn the orchid towards me, to see the card on it. Just what I'd thought. An ordinary orchid from the Co-op, where they keep their plants on display like the picked fruit, too near the door with its draughts and pollution. It looks healthy, still blooming, but give it two weeks. If I had to bet I'd say it's already dead.

A car approaching. A police car. I look up, admiring the stonemasonry. A true Scottish infirmary, my stepfather would say. The car stops near the door to the morgue, and two people get out. The policeman – I know him – but the other man is a stranger. Strange coat. Which reminds me what the old man said of the deceased woman we've come to collect. 'English woman. Up here visiting.'

He hates anything English, John Cattanach, my stepfather. He hated our mum, by the end, and she was half Scottish. There's only one English thing he can stand to be near without going red in the face — redder than natural, his skin vibrating — and that's their money.

'Wait here!' he said. 'Wait. Here.' And I think, standing beside the door to the morgue: this *is* here, *isn't it*? The noise I can hear through the door sounds disturbing. A cat in its death-throes, or something. I push the door open. 'Oh Mum Mum Mum,' I hear, and I realise: not a cat. It's a woman. A woman who's lost all control. 'Mum Mum Mum,' she keeps saying, and sobbing. 'Muuuuuuuummmmm!'

I step into the morgue, slow and solemn, my skin and bones lost in my suit. The surprise is, there's no female present — apart from the one on the table, the dead woman, and her lips are not moving. The voice of despair I was hearing is the voice of this man with the strange overcoat. He's bent over her now, over the dead woman, his hands mostly covering his face.

I take another slow step, towards him, towards his out of control grief. Next to the freezers, three men stand at attention: the policeman, my stepfather and Barry, the morgue manager. All three keep their eyes on the floor, though Barry looks up quickly and winks. My stepfather's eyes are shut tight, his skin close to boiling. If there's one English thing he hates most, it's English outpourings of grief.

Slowly, I step up to the table, thinking to place my hand on the crying man's arm. It seems the right sort of kindness. Then I see the dead woman's face.

My mum's dead and gone. I was there while my stepfather did to her what we do with deceased people, before they get sent to the kiln. Thing is: this dead woman here on the table looks more like my mum did when living than the body we put in her coffin — a body become wasted and shrunken by cancer, shrivelled up almost to nothing. I shiver. What if the whole time we thought she was burnt and in the urn on the shelf, just ashes, these four years now, she wasn't dead, but was somewhere — like back home in Norwich, in our old house, carrying on living without us? I keep it together, mainly by looking away, at the floor, my teeth almost biting my tongue. But then I see her and lose it. I'm crying.

The hand I feel on my elbow is no bringer of kindness. The man in the coat drops his hands and steps back. Before I get tugged into the corridor, I see him. He sees me, up close. The look on his face won't soon leave me. It's a look of horror.

IRIS

I've always had secrets. I'm wrapped in them, layer on layer on layer, it's what I'm made of. I need them. Otherwise there's nothing left for me. The thing about secrets is the spaces they make. Spaces for living, spaces for dreaming, spaces for being. We all need space.

If you hold a secret for a long, long time, it loses its colour and it fades into you. You forget what's true and what's not. You forget what's story and what's real.

I wasn't born Iris, but Barbara, little baby Barbara. I never felt like a Barbara or a Babs, so as soon as I was 18 I grafted a new name for myself. A name I could grow into. Iris. I could have been an Ivy or a Poppy, or a Violet or a Rose. But I chose Iris.

I never told Solomon that.

I wish this kind, strange boy with his dirty tie would bring one of his orchids in here. I can't stand artificial flowers. They make me sneeze. And now there's the rain. I can feel it washing the pain, scrubbing off the layers, rinsing the secrets, one by one, until there's nothing of me left. Nothing left for me.

Well, that was uncomfortable. I sometimes wonder why Agnes and I ever thought turning our home into a business would be a good idea. Lord knows, I like most people and try to be cheerful but there are days when I really feel like kicking everyone out and locking the doors behind them. It's bad enough having to deal with halfwit officials like Lachlan, but having to explain the circumstance of a sudden death to her bereaved children is stretching the idea of hospitality to breaking point.

They're a rum bunch, her children. They obviously knew nothing about why she was here or who she was with. All very uncomfortable. The eldest boy went off with Lachlan to do the identification. He looked like her and had the same way of turning his head sideways when he listened. None of that in the girl. I don't really 'do' teenagers and she reminded me why. Rude, sullen, glued to her phone, casting resentful glances around the hall and drawing room. At one point I was tempted to sit her down, force her to look me in the eye and say, 'I know it is hard and unwelcome, that this house is strange and I am annoying, but, please, listen to me. Your mother is dead, lying on a cold mortuary slab not far from here. In years to come, these moments will be precious to you. Do not waste them.' I didn't, of course. Outwith my remit, as Jock, my old farm manager, used to take great delight in telling me.

The curious one was the younger son, Robin. He seemed semi-detached from the other two. I liked him, for all his lank hair and slightly dozy manner. He did the sensible thing. Poured himself a large dram and sat by the fire.

There's always a fire in the hearth at Balmore, even in the summer months when it barely gets dark. Cheaper than therapy, as one of my London regulars says. It's the heart of the house and a house needs people. That's why we do it, really. Lord knows, it isn't for the money. The prices we charge barely cover the running costs. A house needs a roaring fire; the glow of faces made raw by the bitter winds that rush down off the hill; the clinking of glasses; the glint of silver at dinner; the sound of the fiddle and the *ceòl beag*. It needs songs and whisky to keep it alive or it will end up empty or sold to some faceless banker or oligarch who'll convert it into flats or worse. That's why we do it. It's what my people have always done. Offer protection and provision to all who seek it, the old way of the Highlands.

RICHARD

There's something shifty about this man David Mackintosh. Our 'host' indeed. Give him a moment and he'll regale you with his full name — David Stewart Farquhar Mackintosh — like some ancient laird being piped in to the feast. Not that I'd know. But I do know he seems to be hiding something.

If there's a dial to turn up the heating, he's hidden that. Downstairs in front of the log fire it was cosy but I couldn't stand any more of the forced conversations. 'It's been a long day,' I said. Robin looked absent, Rebecca played with her mobile. I came up to this bedroom and its arctic temperature. There are tall windows with views of snow on the mountains and draughts blowing through the cracks. There's a big double bed you have to climb into and I'll be doing that soon. Best way to keep warm. All around, staring at me, are black-and-white photos of Mackintosh's ancestors. Victorian, Edwardian, soldiers in uniform for this war or that, women holding babies while giving every impression of wanting to hand them on quick to someone else as soon as the camera shutter clicks. The someone else is probably local with an impenetrable accent and a defiant stare — the kind of stare that means 'we'll have no portrait of you in our house'.

Why would Mum want to spend time here? And all by herself? She'd get lonely.

There's no loneliness to compare with being laid out on a mortuary slab. It's a special chill too, one that I've carried back with me to this cold-blooded house. Mum lay there in the hospital morgue, just her face showing, eyes shut but it was her, no mistaking it was her. Her with the breath of life escaped, white-faced, startled, dead. This is not how I want to remember her and I'm scared it will be my abiding memory. When there's so much more to remember. She was a life force, as we'll all say about her, but I can't force her back to life. I'm not even sure I can force back the good memories, the ones I want to keep vivid, the full-colour memories, not the black-and-white portraits.

The cadaverous face of the idiot boy undertaker comes clearest of all to my mind.

I could have been a photographer. I could have been happy recording faces. I never did. Just another missed opportunity in a life full of them. I shouldn't waste this one. What would Mum want me to do? I wish I knew her better but now I know I hardly knew her at all. Perhaps this is my last chance to do what's right for her. As long as Robin and Rebecca don't mess it up.

It niggles me that I don't have her phone. When I asked Mackintosh he looked down at his brogues then up at the antlers on the wall. 'A 19-pointer,' he told me when I followed the direction of his eyes. What? It's a mobile phone I want, not a stag's head. 'That will be a question for the police,' he added.

So I turn out the light and get into bed. The sheets are as white as snow and just as cold. I get out again and put on the socks and vest I'd just discarded. I get extra blankets from the dark-timbered wardrobe. This is going to be a long night.

A long night under the dreams I summon blanket knowing not restful anything they won't be through the night at least some relief comfort blanket of my black bag sleeping pills why Robin looking so curious asleep can I sleep now?

Rebecca White Location: A bog in darkest Scotland. This is DEFINITELY the most bizarre and surreal experience of my life. So I'm in the hotel where mum died, which is freaky enough, but this place is a total mausoleum. The living are massively outnumbered. Every wall has some flaky dead thing nailed to it. In the corridor outside my room there's the head of an antelope. Or a wildebeest or whatever it is. Some horny old f****r. It's got this really surprised look on its face, like it just woke up expecting breakfast on the savannah only to find it's now a disembodied head stuck to a wall in some cold dingy hole in Scotland. There's a crocodile in my room too. It's got beady eyes that follow you around the room like you're trespassing in its swamp. Which is not far from the truth. But the worst is the grizzly bear – it's got DANDRUFF. Don't know how I'll ever get to sleep tonight.
Posted at 23:01pm

Like · Share · Comment

Day 5

WEDNESDAY

RICHARD

Sausages, black pudding, bacon, eggs – even haggis. The breakfast buffet is an invitation to a heart attack but Mum never got as far as the food. I decide to stick to porridge and a sharp apple. This doesn't lighten my mood.

Does the absence of Robin and Rebecca, the lack of sibling banter? No, I'm relieved not to have to talk to them. But at the same time I'm irritated that they haven't yet dragged themselves out of bed. They're supposed to be big enough to know better.

'How are you this morning?' asks Mackintosh. 'I hope you slept well.'

'Too cold to sleep well,' I answer.

'Even with the electric blanket on?'

I crunch into a piece of apple, letting his question drift past me. Embarrassing not to have thought there would be an electric blanket. Of course he could have let me know. But I don't want to give him the satisfaction of putting me down. He leaves me to my porridge and thoughts. I stir them gently with the spoon.

Mackintosh told me that Mum came here every year, then immediately seemed to want to haul back the line he'd spoken. It took me by surprise. I should have pressed him more; I'll talk to him later.

It's a puzzle why Mum should come here once, let alone regularly. She might have known about the electric blankets but it's still a grim grey place where you huddle through icy channels of air between log fire and ancient radiator. The cold reaches into your bones like arthritis.

'Would you like some more tea?'

Drinking hot water will do something for me. Reading *The Times* does very little, but it can be a diversion now that Robin and Rebecca have finally turned up. They sit opposite, Robin's plate heaped with the full fried breakfast, Rebecca nibbling at toast.

We've so little in common. The only thing we share is the same mother, hard to believe but there it is. There's something of Iris in Rebecca's eyes and hair but Robin... Robin's like a genetic aberration. Where did he come from? From the same womb apparently and this, dear Mum, is all I have to say against you. How did you produce a mutant like Robin?

I mustn't. I really must not. What if, against all the agnostic odds, she's looking down on us now from a heavenly cloud? It's not that I'm so God-damn wonderful, I could have done so much better as her son. A good son would have known her love for this place, would have understood it, and probably would have listened when she said she was coming here. Is it the plants? Was that the attraction? *Calluna vulgaris*? Not really at this time of year.

I wish I wish I wish I'd known her better. I wish I hadn't let her down. I wish I'd shared more of her life but I felt she wanted me to live my own life, to be solid in independence. I know Dad did, he never stopped telling me. Mum seemed to fall in with his wishes, perhaps I should have tried harder to see her point of view.

It would be good to find a way of saying goodbye properly.

I'm not sure how... I'm not sure what I mean... but I want to do more than just a funeral service spoken by a priest who never met her. It's too late, of course, but I'd like to meet her, see what she saw in a place like this, watch the world through her eyes. To pay respect. To show I loved her because I didn't do that when she was alive.

'So, brother Rich, what are we going to do?' asks Robin. 'Excellent breakfast. Are we heading back to London?'

Robin has this crass ability to break a train of thought and turn it into a train wreck. I felt I was on the brink there of getting somewhere, but it's gone. Like the man from Porlock knocking on the door and there goes another poem, leaving you grasping after it, trying to catch the mist. I could have been a poet, Mum would have liked that.

I try, then wish I hadn't tried, to say something serious to Robin. To say what I'd been thinking. 'We owe it to Mum.' Robin's eyebrows arch like a cartoon character. His chuckle is Dastardly, or was it Muttley?

Rebecca doesn't even look up from her iPhone. Not even when I ask if she wants to come to the undertaker's and see Mum's body. I'll take her anyway, she can decide for herself when we're there. I'm not her keeper.

And the policeman, we've got to see the policeman.

'Look, just because you're overwhelmed with misery and pain and torment and grief doesn't mean everyone else has to feel the same. She's dead, it's bad, but there it is. Let's just get her back to London and have done with it.'

Richard and I are meeting in the gunroom to discuss his Grand Plan. Certain differences of opinion have emerged.

'"Have done with it"? For God's sake Robin, she was our *mum*. How can "we have done with it"? She's part of who we are. An irreplaceable part.'

He's always like this when he's missed his beauty sleep. And he's always hated the cold. I remember the strops when we went camping as kids.

'Oh for fuck's sake, Rich. Mother had her faults, plenty of them as far as I was concerned. Shouting at me won't change any of that. Now leave me alone, my brain aches.'

It's true. After being granted the freedom of Balmore's drinks cabinet last night I drank not wisely but too well.

'It's all a big joke to you, isn't it? Stumbling along in your own little world, not caring about anything apart from where your next joint is coming from. That and your so-called literary career.' He does that odious air quotes thing, no doubt copied from Julia. 'Can't you be serious, just for once?'

'Why? Why should I be? Don't you see how absurd it all is? She comes to a conference in Scotland and before she's even unpacked her bag she drops dead. No reason, she just does. Because that's how the universe works — random, unfeeling, ridiculous. Of course I fucking laugh, I'd be mad not to. And for your information I've been published just recently. Sort of. That blog could be huge.'

Richard stops pacing, slumps in a chair and exhales loudly. 'We didn't do enough for her.'

Oh no, not The Guilt. Anything but The Guilt. That should be Rebecca's speciality seeing as Mother has handed her over to the God Squad for a 'good old fashioned education'.

Another black mark against her as far as I'm concerned.

'Listen to yourself. What were we supposed to do? We did what all children do — grow up and disappoint their parents. At least I did.'

'Are you saying I haven't grown up? How dare you! I'm a father, a husband and I've got one of the most responsible jobs there is. In fact...'

'Fucking chill out, will you? I'm saying *you* weren't a disappointment to them. It's a compliment. Don't be so paranoid.'

'Oh, well, er, yes, sorry. But I still say we didn't do enough.'

He's calming down, but he's still far too sincere for his own good.

'Rich, that's your grief talking. It's the whole "they're dead but I'm still here" thing. Surely you saw it a hundred times when you were at Barts?'

'That was different. That was other people. That wasn't our mother.'

Please don't cry. Please, PLEASE don't cry. Because if you do I might laugh, and even I can see that would be cruel.

'OK, let's both take a deep breath. Here's what I think. Mother and Father gave us all the stuff anyone could reasonably want, but where was the warmth? The laughs? The fun? It was all study, study, study. Even that wouldn't have been too bad, except half the time she was off giving a paper. And even when she *was* at home she wasn't, if you get me. You know how distant and distracted she used to get, wrapped up in God knows what. Oh I'm sure she loved us, but sometimes she had a funny way of showing it.'

Now who's getting serious and sentimental? Can't have that. I stand up and start buttoning my jacket.

'Look, I'm off out for a walk. It might help my head. We'll work something out, yeah?' I leave Richard sitting there, fingers steepled in front of him, gazing into space and thinking dark thoughts.

REBECCA

Rebecca White @rebwhite   4m
Off to see mother. Wish me luck. Post some pics later.

Rebecca White @rebwhite   7m
Didn't mean THAT. Just from the trip. Not gonna do a
Damien Hearse or something.

Rebecca White @rebwhite   8m
Seriously people? Well… dunno… spose I could…

Christ, what a bunch.

The older lad – buttoned up so tight it makes his head look purple. 'Now look here... ' A right London stiff.

Then there's the lassie. She's not heartbroken. She's not in denial. I reckon she's just numb – or dumb.

And Cock Robin. Maybe the accent's different but the drugs, it's the same smell wherever you go.

None of them have a scoobie really. They didn't even know she was here. The older one's a doctor, though he looks and sounds like an executioner. The original Mr Crabbit. Everything irritates him. He calls me 'officer' but he really means 'my man'. He just wants to know when they can get going.

'The body has been released by the procurator fiscal, and CID have no concerns about her death,' I tell him, 'so you're free to make whatever arrangements you need to make.'

The lassie's gloomy but there's a fair chance she's like this all the time. It's my guess she's sulking at the inconvenience of it all. Just like Mr Crabbit.

Finally I speak to Robin. He's a twitcher. A joker. Wants to show how easy he is with the polis. Always a giveaway. Someone who knows us too well. He's wringing his fingers together, tucking his hands under his armpits, cleaning the dirt from under his nails. On the move all the time and can't wait for this to be over.

'That it then guv?'

'Aye, that's it,' I say.

He grins like it's Hogmanay and strolls off.

With the husband away, the Met suggest it's Mr Crabbit here who should take possession of his mother's belongings. So here they all are, laid out for him to see. It's what we all come down to in the end – just a wee collection of things.

Iris White's is made up of a handbag crammed with credit cards, a miniature bottle of perfume, old photographs, a brown paper bag with three dead flowers inside, an Oyster card, glyceryl trinitrate tablets and a blister pack of paracetamol. Plus a suitcase with all you'd expect for a romantic break in the Highlands: walking clothes, boots, smarter stuff for the evenings, make-up, lingerie, an expensive-looking nightie and a paperback.

'And her phone?' asks Mr Crabbit.

'Er... is it not there?'

Lachlan, you numptie. Of course she would have had a bloody phone. Everyone on the planet has a bloody phone. Where's your head at, man?

'I'll speak to Mr Mackintosh,' I mumble before he can say anything else. 'See if anything's turned up. One of the staff maybe... or perhaps a guest has picked it up.'

My cheeks are burning as I turn away.

So. This is where it happened.

I'm standing in the doorway of Iris's room on Balmore's first floor when I become aware of someone behind me. It's David, our host with the most, wearing what I take to be his 'Ah, what a tragedy' face.

'This was your mother's regular room. Her favourite. Always asked for it. She loved the view of the Strath from here.'

Regular room? How many times had she been here? I somehow assumed this was her first visit; now it seems she practically had her own key. Does Richard know about this?

'Mind if I...?' I gesture inside.

'No, not a bit. We've straightened it up since she, er...'

'Died? Don't panic David, I'm not my sister. We're not all so hyper-sensitive.'

I was trying to reassure him, but he looks unsettled by my sophisticated metropolitan candour. Obviously not the way they do things round here.

We enter. It's large and chilly, with a king-sized bed, wardrobe, a chest of drawers and an elegant escritoire. Everything is super tidy. Unlived in. I can't help wondering who'll be next to sleep here. In that bed. But then they won't know – unless David blabs – so it won't matter.

'Interesting rug,' I nod toward a spatchcocked bearskin complete with snarling head and clawed paws occupying centre stage. Looks like a major trip hazard for anyone stumbling in after dark.

'She, er, Iris, er your mother that is, said she found it amusing, the sort of thing all country houses should have. And our American guests like it. I think my father bought it in Canada years ago, before I took over at Balmore. Not really to my taste, but then this job is all about others. Satisfying their desires.'

His tone seems to add significance to his last remark. Or am I imagining things?

David watches as I poke around. Piles of *Country Life* and *The Field* dating back several centuries. Watercolours of Highland views. A large cartoon of pheasants in tweeds shooting naked male humans driven toward them by grinning gundogs, hilariously entitled 'Go for the cocks'. And, unmissably, several large vases of flowers. There's a rich, almost rotting, scent coming off some pink lilies that's disturbing in the circumstances.

But wait, there must be fifty quid's worth here, maybe more. I can't believe David splashes that sort of cash on every guest. So Mother really was something special to him, and he's just told me she visited Balmore many times. Hold on, *just hold on a minute*, not... *David and Mother*? That's... nah, that's impossible. Entertaining, but impossible.

Still, something's not right. Why *was* she up in Scotland?

And that's a big bed for a small woman.

That policeman. Complete fool. Didn't even occur to him that she might have had a phone, that we might have wanted her phone. It's gone missing. He'll ask Mackintosh (we've done that), the chambermaid, the other guests (there aren't many).

This is the room where she died. It's full of flowers. Real flowers, not just on the wallpaper, curtains and bed covers. The policeman puts Mum's belongings on the bed, in an official plastic bag. 'You'll be wanting these,' the policeman says, and his words draw attention to all the wants that are still missing. Wanting to understand, say goodbye, feel closer. Instead we're left with a suitcase, a handbag, their contents such a light weight for a life that meant such a lot.

But it's something at least. In the absence of better, we can look through what she brought, what she left. I do my best to put on a professional demeanour as I sift through my mother's dresses, cardigans, underwear, wash bag. Then deeper into her life and handbag, her purse, keys, cosmetics, tablets, photographs.

These photographs. None of me or any of the family. But four pictures of places. Buildings set in trees or gardens. One of them is here, it's the house seen from the lawn below. The trees are bare but you can see daffodils. I turn it over to find, written in Mum's handwriting, the words 'My favourite house for a Scottish spring.'

There's a picture of an Oxford college. I'd never know which one but she's written 'Merton College' and 'Favourite for winter' on the back.

The next one is an Arts and Crafts house. It's a period I like, look at the terraces and the roof. The writing on the back tells me it's in the Lake District and the summer favourite.

The final one shows an Indian man dressed in chef's uniform. 'The Peak Boutique' it says on the back 'for autumn'.

I don't know what to make of them. It seems clear that these are places close to Mum's heart but I find it hard to look at them sentimentally. It feels, as I examine them, like something is opening up underfoot, a chasm into which I might fall. I sit down on the bed.

'Cool,' says Rebecca. It's the first time she's spoken this morning and now I wish she hadn't. Whatever I'm feeling it's not *cool*. It's all a bit much. Why these places?

'She's the sly one,' says Robin. 'Sneaking off and abandoning her poor children.' There are more things in heaven and earth, Robin, than are dreamt of in your philosophy. I see no reason to imagine anything sly. I just wish she'd shared these places with us when she was alive.

But it's a thought. Can she share them with us now? Can we share them with her? She's pointed us towards the places.

'I wonder where they are,' I say aloud. Rebecca has her iPhone open and within minutes we know exactly where they are. Head south of here, then south again, and again. A journey in little hops. Mackintosh would probably shoot it and stuff it.

I leave the room, it's suddenly oppressive. I feel uncomfortable turning over these secret stones of Mum's life. Innocent, of course. She was a refined woman, she loved places that were not just interesting, they were more, they had stories attached. Shouldn't we learn and tell the stories? Fiction's in the DNA of this family. But is that prying? The notion of patient confidentiality pops into my head. Ridiculous, she wasn't my patient, I've a right to know more. And she has a right to have respects paid, to be honoured, to connect with places that were special to her — and that could be special for me. Is this spying?

I could have been a spy living a life of intrigue not tedium. I could have been a detective solving puzzles in the lives of others, exposing the secret affairs of lovers, putting right the wrongs that lurk behind the double-glazed windows of suburbia. But I'm neither spy nor detective. Instead I treat the common colds and coughs and sneezes with placebos until one day with the passing of years the underlying suspicion gets strong enough to point the finger at a cancer, not a cough and the cancer points at death. And that's the inevitable end of what I do. I'm a doctor diagnosing death. It all leads to that. We toddle we run we walk we stroll we stagger we crawl until all we can do is lie in a hospital's terminal bed.

At least Mum avoided that. But you have to let it play out in its own time and place. Let it run its course in the way nature intended. Like Mum understood with plants, they have a cycle, they sway to the rhythm of sun and moon and seasons. Not like Robin, with his contempt for the natural, the pursuit of the synthetic. I want to use this time to get closer to things that mattered to Mum because they should matter to me. And Robin, and Rebecca.

I can't say that, of course, without risking Robin spluttering into a Robin rant or Rebecca retreating into a sulk. So I keep it to myself. But Mum would have understood.

REBECCA

Why must you be so cruel to me H? Don't say things like that. I want it more than anything. Whatever the price, that's what we said. And I know you have the most to lose but I just have to get through this. It will be soon I promise.

iMessage, 20 Mar 2013 21:24

So anyway, weird thing, found these pictures in mum's stuff. Pictures of places. Like natural scenes, but not the close-ups she always takes. She's written on the back that they're her favourite places for the different seasons. Were… but weve never been to any of them.

iMessage, 20 Mar 2013 21:26

She never even MENTIONED them to me. Not once. And these are her favourite places. The freaky thing is I don't think she even took these pictures. Just not her style.

iMessage, 20 Mar 2013 21:27

So WHO DID? And what are these places? Well get this, one is this dump. FAVOURITE PLACE???? Are you KIDDING ME???????!!!!!!!!

iMessage, 20 Mar 2013 21:30

PHILIP

Where is he? And who are they? They're still here — and everyone's saying they are her children! But he said he didn't have any. Mum said I must have been mistaken — and she said the skinny one with long hair looked like him, had the same nose, she said — but I'm not mistaken, I'm really truly not. He *told* me.

And it really was her who died because I saw her! Where is he? And who *are* they?

It never occurred to me that it would end up like this. It is turning into quite a mess. Iris's mobile phone has mysteriously disappeared, which has added considerably to my sense of embarrassment and awkwardness with the family. I didn't notice it at the time and only Janet would have been in there after the body had been taken. She swears blind she never saw it. Though we do at least know that Iris had one. When Janet was doing the evening turndown she happened to overhear her speaking on it in her room. Be that as it may, I really don't like telling lies but I can't explain its disappearance. I've upbraided that fool policeman Lachlan but he has no record of it. Simply didn't think to look — which meant me sounding like a bloody idiot as I explained myself to the rather pompous elder son. Not altogether successfully, I might add.

Still, at least I've finally spoken to Angus — though for the sake of discretion I don't mention his name to anyone. Poor man — he's back in London but sounded utterly bereft. I can't imagine what it must be like for him. Being held up on his way here, knowing how upset she was about it — at least that seemed to be the tenor of the phone conversation Janet overheard — then learning from me next morning that she was dead, that the children were on their way, and that it would be best for everyone if he simply went home. Now he just has to sit on his hands and express his condolences to the family. Agony, I should imagine. And, like I say, a proper mess.

I never really understood why they went to the bother of all the cloak and dagger stuff. They were so obviously right for one another, so clearly in love. I've known Angus since we were boys. Utterly wild, utterly charming. The years in the States, the death of his first wife, mellowed him, rubbed off some of the corners. But he's still a ladies' man, brimming with the kind of charm people don't normally associate with Scotsmen. He's good looking too, with a knack for striking canny business deals, so naturally when he first brought Iris to Balmore, we assumed she would be just one in a long line of conquests. Not at all. She was so elegant, so witty and he was so obviously besotted with her, coming to Balmore became their spring ritual. For more than a decade, he never came here without her.

I got to know her well. She knew the trees and flowers up on the hills better than anyone. I remember her once showing me a saxifrage she'd gathered on the summit of Ben Macdui – it was exquisite, with small white flowers. Me, a Highlander who spent most of his life on the hills, had never seen it before. It was called *Saxifraga caespitosa* – the Tufted Alpine Saxifrage and it only grew in the highest and most inaccessible places. That's what I liked about Iris: she was slight and quiet, but determined and intrepid. She looked at the world more closely than other people. She had a way of getting what she wanted. And what she seemed to want most of all was Angus.

Perhaps that's why I'm so protective of them. I'm hardly a natural advocate for adultery. I dislike the slack-jawed, screen-addicted, phone-dependent, morally-messy society we've degenerated into. Inventing stories and telling half-truths doesn't come easily to me – 'Your word is your bond, Davey was my father's favourite bit of wisdom, and I have tried to live by it. But they seemed to belong to an older, more beautiful world. They remind me of a couple in a medieval romance, with their rituals, their flowers and their unembarrassed passion for one another. Or, rather, they did. They were my friends, and if a cantankerous Scotsman who drinks too much whisky and used to spend too much time blasting birds out of the sky is still capable of love, I suppose I loved them.

Here is what I know about the heart.

I know that *Dicentra formosa* bleeding heart is poisonous. I know that *Digitalis purpurea* foxglove, planted near the compost heap, slows the heart rate down. I know that when a tree is cut down, adjacent trees put out an electric pulse. It looks like the beat of a human heart.

When Angus told me he loved me, my heart flew away. He clasped my face (as if I would ever bolt from him!), and I was lifted into peace. It was the hope that caught me, grasping at tendrils of a promised life when we were together. He called me *Gra mo chree* – 'Love of my heart.' Back home in London I wondered if I'd been dreaming. This life of ours, that was almost mine.

I know that I love Angus with my whole heart.

I know that before Angus, I believed my heart was too full of the children to love anyone else. But I forgot that the human heart is made of muscle. But I did not know that my heart would stop beating. I did not know that my heart was so broken. I did not know that my heart could keep breaking. I did not know that when a broken heart breaks, it brakes, brakes, breaks. It breaks and now I am broken.

Day 6

THURSDAY

Parents of teenagers are always telling me that their children are endlessly available to their friends by text, Facebook chat, or even — the horror — by speaking on their mobiles, but that should they, the doting mother or father, try and contact their progeny, the ever-living device is mysteriously inactive. You'd imagine it wouldn't be true of grown children, but I've tried phoning each of them and it's gone straight to voicemail. None of the messages have been returned, not even a miserable text.

I can excuse Rebecca, as a fully paid-up teenager and non-acknowledger of any grown-up except Iris. (God, every time her name goes through my mind, a scream goes through the centre of my being.) And I'm almost prepared to excuse Robin. Speed dial has a different meaning for him.

But Richard. What is he up to? The saintly Julia, my umbilical-cord-in-law to my own offspring, tells me that mobile reception is dodgy up there, and she's been struggling to get through to him too. But I can tell that she is only being diplomatic and besides, she hasn't denied that she *has* spoken to him. I've given her my hotel landline, and she's promised to pass it on to Richard. There'll be landlines in the Highlands too, I shouldn't wonder. Anywhere civilised enough to make malt whisky will have telephones. When I think of the support I gave Mum when Dad died, it makes me sick. Even if I'm reaping what I've sown, there comes a moment when you put that to one side in the interests of pulling together as a family.

Well, sod 'em, all three of them. I've got troubles of my own here, not that they give a shit. The least of it is trying to get a flight back to London. It would be easier to swim the English Channel underwater with my hands tied behind my back. If it wasn't for the nagging fear of what the hell is going on back there, I'm not sure I'd have the stamina. I'd have a private ceremony of remembrance for Iris here, visit the places we went to together, and remember her, and for that matter us, at our very best. It would be vastly more meaningful than the compromised charade that a family funeral is bound to turn into.

And, lying here on my creaking hotel bed, I'm more or less coiled into the embryo position thinking about the lecture. What an utter, abject catastrophe. My first ever keynote address, and I end up blubbing like a child and being led off the stage by Felicia Esteban. What was I thinking of?

But of course, I was thinking of you, wasn't I, Iris? How did I not see it coming, how did I think I was going to get through that reminiscence of coming to Cuba on our honeymoon and not dissolve into a puddle at the podium? For sure, there are excuses. I hadn't bothered to re-read the contents of the lecture, what with you dying and the trauma of trying to reorganise my flight. So there I was, up there in front of the audience, blinking out at them in the glare of the lights, when the forgotten words about our honeymoon swam into view. And that was it. All the conflicting thoughts and emotions of the past few days, essentially an expanded symphony from the overture of the first half an hour after the call from Julia, fell away in a primal howl of pain for losing you.

Even that wasn't the worst of it. All of that was predictable, and forgivable. What came next was neither. Felicia, with her big hearted Cuban compassion, decided to take me out of public view. As conference organiser, she had a room in the conference hotel, and she took me up there, in order to let me recover in peace and quiet. It was a small room, and she ushered me to perch on the end of her bed. I sat still, an incongruous blend of numb nothingness and violent grief, while she bustled around, fetching me a drink and a small packet of tissues.

Felicia said that she had to go back down and see to the set-up of the next session. She promised she'd come back and check on me in a little while. I was just about to let her go when, on impulse, I stopped her.

'Felicia, don't go. Can you stay for a while?'

'Solomon?' She inclined her head towards me in a quizzical way.

'I could use the company right now.'

'Do you want to talk?' For a split second she looked torn, but then fifteen years of working camaraderie kicked in and she came and sat down beside me. 'They know what to do. Let them get on with it.'

'The thing is...'

Whatever I had been planning to say, and I have no idea what it was, never came out. The tears started again. Felicia pulled my head into the crook of her shoulder and I made no attempt to resist. From where I was nestled, I had nothing in my field of vision other than Felicia's magnificent, cinnamon-scented cleavage. I watched a couple of tears that had dropped off my chin run down the gap between her breasts. I shocked myself by feeling envious of my tears, scouting around down there, the only part of me to have intimate contact with another woman's breasts for over thirty-five years. How could a thought like that occur to me at such a moment? I felt Felicia become aware of them, maybe they were tickling her, because she stirred and changed position. I offered her my tissue, stained with less fortunate tears, which she accepted. She dabbed away at the salty rivulet and caught me looking. She blushed and we both giggled.

'I'm sorry,' I stammered.

'What for?'

'Oh. Well. You know.' Articulate to the last, more sliver tongued than silver tongued, I had a sudden jolting memory of trying to ask out Janice Barker in my O-level year.

Maybe the remembrance of my inaction back then was an influence. Who knows? But the next thing I knew I was kissing Felicia. I'd love to report that it was horrific and appalling, but in fact it was sweet and wonderful. Somehow Iris's death and transition into the kingdom of the dead had rebooted me into the kingdom of the living. For a few seconds Felicia kissed back and I willingly surrendered myself to anything that might happen. But, thank God, she pulled back and stopped.

'Solomon, I'm sorry. This is so wrong.'

'You're right. It's me that is sorry. I'm not in my right mind. I don't know whose mind I am in.'

'Solomon, look. These things happen. It is all right. But now I really should get back to the conference.'

I nodded my agreement, not trusting myself to speak and watched her retreating figure as she composed herself and adjusted her hair before leaving, without looking back.

So was it like that for you, Iris, the first time? A feeling of exciting transgression? Kissing Felicia is the only time it's ever happened to me, and, strictly speaking, there was no harm in it. She is single, and so, according to the letter of the law, am I. Of course, I don't feel single, I feel permanently married to you. But you didn't, did you? There was no proof, no certainty, you were brilliant at covering your tracks, or at least I never wanted to find any evidence. And as time went by, the blatant regularity of your absences became almost reckless. Without anything ever having been said between us, you'd worked out that I knew and that therefore I wasn't going to call you on it. Did I ever intend to? I'm not sure. Certainly my window passed. There came a point where I was morally complicit. And in the early days, I was so dazed and hurt, that for all the times I rehearsed the conversation, I had no idea how to broach it. The words wouldn't come. I hoped it would blow over. But it never did. I can only assume it has been the same man. Had it been a sequence of liaisons, the regularity wouldn't have been there. Is that better or worse? I've no idea. I'd need to talk to you about it. But you've left me for good this time.

How dare you? And how dare I have let you go?

REBECCA

This place is doing my head in. Not to mention the fam. Dads still sunning himself in the Caribbean. Robin never comes out of his room and has said like five words to me the whole time.

Dishwaters behaving weirdly. Pacing around and muttering under his breath. Saw him arguing with Robin in the car park last night. Waving his arms and everything, proper furious. Asked him about it today and he said it was none of my business. Charming.

Thought it was mum's masterstroke sending me to a catholic school. But no, she's managed to drag me somewhere even worse. Even though shes dead she still has to torture me.

RICHARD

I'm looking at the AA road map on my laptop. And thinking it might be possible. It's just 258 miles from here to Hartley Hall in the Lake District. The AA says it will take only five hours to drive.

I'm sure Mum would like to be there one last time, even if it's slightly out of season for her. I want to see it, feel what it's like. And share that with her.

I raise the possibility with Robin and Rebecca. Robin looks at me as if I'm mad but that's normal. I do the diagnoses, not you, Robin. Rebecca, of course, says nothing. Anyway, the seed is planted. I open up my doctor's bag, check what's there, just to make sure I'm the medical authority here, I'm in charge of life and death. I take out: thermometer, tongue depressors, stethoscope, reflex hammer, syringes, morphine, antibiotics, tranquillisers, sleeping pills, antihistamines, adrenaline. Just checking. The travel supplies of a GP, unlikely to need any of it, but you never know.

I take a bath. The bathtub wouldn't win any awards at the Ideal Home Show but the water's hot. For the first time since arriving, I feel a little warmth seeping into my bones. Getting out, though, you don't want to hang around in this chilly bathroom. I put the coarse white towel over my head and rub my scalp gently. I'm not pleased to see so many strands of my hair on the towel, and I shake it to get rid of them. In the mirror, combing carefully, I stare at a drawn face.

I'm not feeling good, doctor.

I can see that.

I prescribe myself a little something from my bag. Just to help me through the day. My day involves Robin, Rebecca, the undertaker and Mackintosh. Enough to make anyone feel below par. But, though it pains me, I need these people on my side.

I kill time by looking through the magazines on the bedside table: lots of hunting, shooting and fishing, plus a few women's titles. I'm appalled by the content of the latter, especially by one front-page headline that invites you inside to read about 'LOOSE WOMEN HOOKED ON YOUNGER MEN'. Appalled and offended on Mum's behalf.

ROBIN

Richard's just been explaining his plan for a magical mystery tour of the British Isles to me. It sounds entertaining enough but raises an important question, namely, what am I supposed to do for supplies? I was low on weed when I left London, and even limiting myself to a couple of smokes on the terrace after dark means I'm down to the dust in the bottom of the bag. Even that'll be gone soon. Now it seems we're taking the long route home and that means trouble. What to do?

Option One — go without. Quite impossible. A week or more stuck in a van with my dead mother, brain-dead brother, twisted sister and a local member of the Addams Family calls for something strong to smoke. Any reasonable person would agree.

Option Two — shop locally. That means a visit to The Claymore. It's risky but no worse than buying in The Black Bear. I doubt anyone in The Claymore is actually armed.

Option Three — ask Adie to post something up. Forget it. Entertaining though he is, Adie can barely wipe his own bottom, let alone get it together to buy a stamp.

Option Four — run away home. It's always worked before. Still, I'll keep that in reserve until things get really bad.

That's that, then. It looks like the middle class Londoner with a considerable quantity of cash in his pocket will be visiting a rough looking pub in an unknown Highland village in an effort to locate the local drug laird. What could possibly go wrong?

CALLUM

Welcome to my refuge, I say to myself, closing the door of my bedroom. *Welcome to the lair.* And I laugh in a private way that I have, which is not really laughing. The plants show no sign of caring about any of this.

I breathe in and breathe out, relaxing. This *is* my refuge, always has been. 'Callum Callum Callum,' the others would say, before school started, and during it. 'He sucks his teeth and keeps to hisself. He's nought but bones, and he smells like death.' They never said such of my brother Corey, maybe because he was a good footballer, and a good talker, who stepped out of the estate car we had then with a football aloft, talking like a Badenoch native, seeming to enjoy it, as if his whole life up to then had been one long, cramped act of ventriloquism.

I sniff my skin. It smells of soap, no whiff of the work I was doing all morning, holding the old man's utensils, following his orders, emptying buckets. I sniff my skin again and am less certain. The odours can get into your pores, your clothes. But mainly they get into your skull.

I pull my shirt off, glimpsing myself in the parts of the mirror that aren't blocked by my biggest Alocasia plant, my Yucatan Princess. Not for the first time, I see in my ribcage the pattern of a strange albino leaf, with my arm as its stem.

'That dead Englishwoman,' I said to the old man during our tea break. 'Deceased', he said, his mouth full of scone. 'Aye,' I said, 'but didn't you think...' I tried to say it. He looked up at me, waiting, but I couldn't. I couldn't mention my mum to this man. 'Did you not think she...' I tried again, and I nodded, letting my eyes try to say what I meant. He tightened the clamp of his lips. For a second we seemed to be seeing the same possibility, the same mystery. He stood up. 'Show some deference', he said, smacking the back of my head. He helped himself to a third scone.

I'm about to cross the hallway to the bathroom, to get my deodorant, when the bell rings downstairs. The postman's already rung, so it has to be customers. I turn on the little viewing screen in the hallway, activating its camera – not to be creepy, just to be certain the old man is down there and will see to them. I watch him – a grainy big man on a tiny screen – shuffle his way through the shop, a finger probed into his mouth, picking at something. I know what that something is, too: he's been in the closet next to the office, scoffing down Wagon Wheels from a jar that he keeps there, behind the unclaimed cartons of ashes, a stash he thinks I'm not wise to.

I can't see the old man's face when the door opens, but I can picture it, easy: the face of total deference, but redder. The Englishwoman's son stands in the doorway, shivering, arms wrapped round himself, like a self-made straitjacket. For a long moment, my stepfather looks towards the door to the stairs, where I am, probably wishing I'd come down and stand near him. It gives him a boost to be seen to have help.

The son cocks his head and another appears in the doorway, moving so quick, this way and that, I can barely see him. The two of them step in to the shop, and here comes a third one, a girl, still in school by the look of her — younger than me.

John Cattanach does his funeral-director nod at the three of them and trundles back to the office, maybe to get the keys to our tiny chapel. The phone rings, and he answers it. For a minute or more I watch three people — three Londoners — each looking uncomfortable in their different ways, not knowing quite what to do with themselves in a room full of empty coffins and blank gravestones.

The first man, the one from the hospital morgue, stands where he landed, right by the door, shivering. But the girl, who might be his daughter, wanders in further, stops at the shelf with the leaflets for pre-planned funeral packages. But she's not looking at those. It's the picture of my brother she's seeing, the picture he sent instead of coming home from university last Christmas, which the old man framed and put on show, like an example of a personal memorial. The girl looks at it, at my brother, who's smiling out at her, I know, happy on a balmy long beach in southwest England — his hair wet. He would be smiling, too, because he's not here.

The other man, whose age I can't tell — though he's skinny like me; maybe skinnier — is a streak of quick movements, one big twitch, which I take to be tied to his grief. He lifts the lid on a coffin, pats down the satin. Within seconds, he's spotted the camera. At first he seems wary, stealing glances. Then he looks right up into it, a big eye on the wall in my hallway. His face disappears, reappears, smaller. And I see a hand that gets bigger, two hands, fingers twirling and crazy, all ten fingers, looking more like fifteen. Then nothing. Static.

So how do we get Mother's mortal remains back to civilisation? Our friendly family undertaker Mr Cattanach is in favour of us using a specialist service based in Inverness. A bit too in favour if you ask me.

'Aye, they're professionals. True professionals, Mr Hannett and Mr Grieve. Discreet, reliable. dependable. The last time I used them was for a resident of Manchester. They got him home without a hitch.'

Which isn't exactly surprising, all they had to do was find the fucking M6 South. Do I detect the sweet smell of kickback beneath the odour of embalming fluid?

In the other corner is Richard with his ambitious — some might say grandiose — plan for a multi-car funeral cortège all the way from here to Turnham Green. I'm only surprised he hasn't suggested a horse-drawn hearse, black ostrich plumes all round and professional mourners lining the route. And he calls me a dreamer.

The flaw in both schemes is obvious — money. The Inverness corpse couriers want £1,800 for their troubles, while the cortège option is well over two grand. And let's face it, Iris is past caring; it's we the living who feel this particular aspect of death's sting.

'So John, is there any way we can ask Mr Hannett and Mr Grieve to sharpen their pencil?'

He looks at me sternly. But then I get the impression he looks at everyone sternly.

'I don't follow you.'

'Make some saving, reduce their fee.'

'Och, I wouldn't have thought so. Theirs is a dependable, reliable...'

'...discreet service, yes, so you said.' *Makes them sound like an upmarket escort agency.* 'Can't we at least ask?'

'There's no point, I know the answer in advance. It's not the first time I've dealt wi' them.'

Hmm, and it's not the first time you've copped an envelope of notes in return. No thanks. I turn to Richard.

'Look Rich, it's just too much. And your idea, well, it's even worse — there's no point looking at me like that, it is — almost two and a half thousand quid to be driven home. It's outrageous.'

He knows I'm right. He might be daft but he's not stupid. 'So what do you suggest?'

'Well, what's to stop us doing it ourselves? Christ, we'll be home in 12 hours if we stop pissing about.'

Cattanach makes an ostentatious show of disapproval at my language. He's the nut I need to crack.

'Why can't your assistant drive us back in your big Transit? There's plenty of room in there for the five of us.'

The way he widens his eyes and turns down the corners of his mouth you'd think I'd just suggested we stock up on poppers and hit the local gay bar.

'No, no, no, quite out of the question. No, impossible.'

'But why?'

'It... just is. Callum, my stepson, he's...'

'But it's not a legal thing, is it? You said yourself, with a signed release form we're safe as fuck — *that frown again* — and we're her family, and he's a doctor.'

'Look I'm sorry, Mr White but...'

'Obviously we'll pay for Callum's time and for hiring the van. Handsomely.' I've always liked the idea of 'paying handsomely'. Never said it before. It feels good.

'It's not the money, it's...'

'How about 500 quid?'

Pause. Ah, so it's not 'not the money'. It's just a question of how much.

'No, I couldn't...'

'Oh but I think you could. If we offered you enough.

Look Mr Cattenback...'

'Cattanach.' His disgust at my character, my accent, my nationality and my whole existence is unmistakable.

'Yes, Mr Cattanach, I tell you what, let's stop messing about.' *Man to man isn't my natural territory but I'll give it a go.* 'Richard, Rebecca and I want to get our dear mum home to London — *blessed London* — without incurring unnecessary costs. You have the means for us to do it. Surely there's a deal to be done? I thought you Scots were a canny lot.' There's nothing like invoking racial stereotypes to seal a deal.

'Oh you want canny do you? Aye, well, maybe I can oblige you there.' He pauses and puffs out his chest in a way I imagine he thinks is imposing. Instead he looks like an angry little bully. 'It's going to cost you 750, plus the petrol, and I want Callum and the van back here in three days, d'you hear?'

Richard and I exchange glances. We'll be far longer than that but once we're on the road Cattanach can go fuck himself.

'Done.' I hold out my hand and after a second's delay Cattanach shakes it. Where's that hand been? What's it touched just today? Ugh, don't Robin, think happy thoughts. Like, 'We're going home tomorrow'.

PHILIP

We're going home tomorrow. I go to put her phone back in her room but someone else is in it now. What am I going to do with it? I can't give it to them. They'll think I stole it. They might find out I went into her room.

I'm thinking I might give it to that girl — if she's really her daughter then she'll want it, won't she? But she's like one of those horrible bitchy girls at school who think they're so cool but are really just mean. They sit in the playground chewing gum and texting all the time and sneering at us because our mums won't let us have our own phones yet.

I can't give it to her. And anyway, who is she? Who *are* they?

And he's *still* not here. Maybe he died too. Maybe she killed herself. Maybe he killed himself. Maybe they're both dead. That must be why he isn't here. He must be dead too.

Maybe I should tell the policeman they're not her children. But then they'll find out about the phone, and they'll say I stole it because I've had it for three days. I can't tell them.

I know, I'll leave it in that elephant's foot waste-paper basket thing near her room. And they'll just think she dropped it. That's what I'll do. I'll put it in the elephant's foot.

I will keep my secrets to myself. Telling them that their mother loved another man is hardly going to help with funeral preparations. As they glumly ate their meal this evening — some rather good Balmore venison, not particularly appreciated — I was struck by how ill-sorted they seem. But for the fact that they all shared the same mother, you'd barely know they were related. And the more I see of Robin, the more I wonder... Despite the general slovenliness, he has more spirit in him than the others. It's not impossible — Iris's marriage wasn't happy, that much I knew. And it seems odd to me that the father isn't here or even much discussed. Surely he should be in charge, the chief mourner, offering his children succour and love in their hour of need?

But what do I know? I've noticed this often about the English over the years: their sense of family allegiance is weak, perhaps because it no longer matters as much as professional status or wealth. Being a Mackintosh has more or less defined my life. I may be from a minor branch of the Clan, but I was brought up on the stories, as were my father and grandfather before me. There's barely a battle in the long history of the Highlands that doesn't feature some Mackintosh or other, in our great feud against the Camerons. As a boy I knew the names of all of the skirmishes: Largs, Bannockburn, Drumlui, North Inch, Harlaw, Lochaber, Inverlochy, the disaster at Glenlivet, the raid on Ross, the rout of Moy. And how the Mackintoshes rallied to the Clan Chief's wife and were the first to charge the Hanoverians at Culloden and almost all perished in the process. These stories are what fired me as a child and have sustained me through the long years of trying to keep this ancient house alive. When I put on my grandfather's old wild cat sporran — utterly illegal now, of course — with the crest and motto 'Touch not the cat bot a glove', I know who I am. I am David Stewart Farquhar Mackintosh, laird of Balmore, member of the great Clan Mackintosh, whose men and women have fought, loved and mourned across these hills for nearly a thousand years.

How long will that last? Will my sons really want to struggle with a house that always costs more to run than it can ever earn back? Or an estate with sour soil that only grows heather and game? All you can do is your best, as my father loved to say.

I watched them eat and felt sorry for them, and even more sorry for Angus. And cross too. He and Iris should have known that deceit is always wrong. And they have made me part of theirs. But my ties to Angus are deep. He helped me once when it looked like I would lose Balmore.

Their secret is safe with me.

Rebecca White Read my mum's horoscope today. Don't
know why really. This is what it said. Freaky cos we are going
on a trip.

'Your selfless attitude may have led you to take too much
upon yourself lately. But good news – travel is on the cards,
perhaps a family holiday or outing. You've been dying to escape
for ages, so be sure to get the rest and peace you deserve.
Let others handle the arrangements. Just chill, and allow
yourself to be spoiled rotten.'
Posted at 21:55pm

Like · Share · Comment

Rebecca White My mother is a Pisces.
Posted a few seconds ago

Like · Share · Comment

From: Rebecca White
To: Iris White
Subject: Hello?

Hi mum. This is stupid. I'm not going to send this. Or I will, just on
the off chance you can actually read email. This is so ridiculous. But
I'll go in and delete it so no one ever finds out I actually emailed my
dead mother. God this is so weird. And yes, I did hack your email
account. Just the work one, you were obviously more careful with
your gmail password. And yes, that's how I knew about your dialogue
with the school and your plans to pack me off. Why mum? Can't
anything be innocent? It won't stop us. Please just let me be.

PS Are you there?
PPS Don't know why I'm doing this. It's just a stupid fantasy.
But DON'T REPLY!!!

Needless to say the dart stopped in mid air as I walked in. The Claymore is that kind of place. Parochial. Suspicious. Vile. I thought The Black Bear was bad but the sight of two mongrels shagging by the cigarette machine surpasses anything I've seen in my south London local. People shagging, certainly. But dogs? They're barred.

Just as I'm struggling to get the attention of the dead-eyed girl behind the bar a group of youths enter emitting a strong whiff of what I'm after. Baseball caps high on foreheads, trackie bottoms tucked into socks – standard issue scum. They head for the pool table and noisily begin a game. I give it five minutes then walk over to put down my money.

One look is enough. 'English.' A statement not a question.

'Yes. You up for a game?'

'Aye, why not? Mebbe settle a few old scores.'

That doesn't sound too promising. Nor do the hard stares and sharp elbows during the first shots. But I persevere, making small talk and buying pints, until half an hour later I'm seeing a whole other side to these Highland lowlife.

'...so you see Robin, the 1707 Act o' Union was forced on Scotland in response to the financial crisis triggered by the failure o' the Darien adventure. Not so much a marriage o' convenience as one born o' dire financial necessity.'

Hamish, the leader of the pack, is leaning on his pool cue, our game forgotten, as he outlines the finer points of Scotland's geo-economic oppression.

'But Hamie...' counters a ferret-faced youth, '...you'll surely no deny it was a crisis o' our own makin' as the fledgling Scottish nation strove tae create an imperial base that would enable us to compete wi' the nascent British Empire.'

Hamish raises his cue threateningly and glares at his companion. 'Pish! How many times do I have to tell you, Alex, it were an arrangement foisted on the population by a risin' mercantile class in bed wi' London and eager for access to overseas markets!'

The smallest youth, introduced to me as Ratty, mutters to no one in particular, 'As Rabbie Burns wrote, *We are bought and sold for English gold. Such a parcel of rogues in a nation.*'

And with that my hosts are overtaken by a collective gloom, frowning into their pints as they silently consider what Scotland is and might have been. I need to get things back on track.

'So, about the weed...?'

My voice rouses Hamish from his reverie. 'Eh? Have you no heard a word we've said? *Bought and sold for English gold.* Yous lot are still at it!'

Comparing England's eighteenth-century colonial expansion to my search for something to smoke seems a tad excessive, but I'm not about to argue. Thankfully I have a trump card up my sleeve (or rather in my sock).

'Look Hamish, I've a suggestion that might make amends for my nation's economic imperialism. I'm talking about fair trade conducted in an atmosphere of mutual respect for our reciprocal benefit. You might be interested to hear that my brother's a doctor. You might be even more interested to hear what I found in his medical bag this evening.'

That got their attention.

'Such as?'

'Diazepam. 10mg tablets. Full bottle. Must be sixty there. Not my cup of tea but I bet there's a ready market round here.'

And so it was that nation spake peace unto nation. I got my weed plus a few speckled pills stamped with the Apple logo thrown in 'as a gesture o' fraternity between our two great countries', Hamish and his acne-ridden entourage got Rich's valium and fifty quid to make up the difference. If only all international relations could be conducted so agreeably.

Day 7

FRIDAY

CALLUM

A knock on my door. It's the old man, giving me the keys to the van. 'Callum,' he says and draws breath. His eyes bulging, his face fairly red. He says it again. 'Callum.' I know what he means without hearing it, because he's said it already, three times.

Show some deference. Don't be a scunner. Don't waste any time, going or coming. Don't wreck my van.

That accident the last time – he knows as well as I do it wasn't my doing. The other car came out of nowhere. The cardboard box was banged up, but the body inside it was fine. And the other accident was a freak of nature. The old man knows well as anyone, there's no accounting for ice.

He looks over my shoulder, into my room, at my plants. He's never liked plants, never even pretended he did. He draws a breath, holds it. 'And change your tie,' he says. 'It's got egg white all up it.' The phone rings, and I stand looking at the keys, my skin itching. In the other room, he answers it. 'John Cattanach Funeral Director,' he says, using a voice that couldn't be more put-on and soothing if it was Sean Connery's.

I close my door and look round the room, at my plants. I've amassed a collection, some fairly rare, and some that I've brought back from a bad way, a way so bad that most would have thought it couldn't be helped. *What will you do while I'm gone*? I say to them all. *What will you do without Daddy*? And I laugh my private laugh.

My bag is packed. I have quarter of an hour left, which I use doing all that I can – spraying the plants that need spraying, giving fishmeal to some that need that. I walk past the Lesser-Butterfly orchid and its tent and grow lamp at least three times before noticing: stalk with tiny buds coming out.

I've done it – I've forced a live plant into blooming four months earlier than natural. I pick up the pot, and we dance. The stalk looks ready but fragile, each row of buds like tiny, premature arms reaching out. *No wonder your kind are endangered*, I say, shaking my head.

Never mind the dangers you'd have had, if...

I don't finish the rest. Maybe I can't. Or don't want to − don't want to think of what might have become of my orchid if it had stayed on in that rusting conservatory in Grantown, after we'd wheeled out the deceased − whose nieces and nephews would have been too busy fighting to think of caring for her plants, even this one.

I wrap the pot in kitchen foil, to protect it, and I slide it down into my bag. It looks strange, this, an overnight bag with a wild Highland plant sticking out. I laugh, or I try to, feeling sad for some reason but also glad − glad that I took it.

IRIS

It is possible to judge the purity of the air by how much lichen is growing on the trees. In the woodlands near the Lakes, the trees are covered in lichen as if they've been touched by magical frost. Waiting for Angus, I would fill my notebook with drawings of handsome Specklebellies (*Pseudocyphellaria species*) and Blackberries and Custard (*Parmentaria chilense*). Since we've been coming here, I've recorded 182 different species.

Is life like air? Can you judge the quality of a life, the purity of life by what grows on you? When they cracked me open to look at my broken heart (ha!), did they find blankets of *Catolechia wahlenbergii*, swards of *Racomitrium lanuginosum*? Or was it barren, a wasteland?

How do you know if someone is leading a good life or a bad life? Is it quantified by the quality of work they produce, the happiness of their children, the length of their marriage, the width of their smile? When they cracked me open, to look at my broken heart, what did they see?

Hurtling down the M74 in a decrepit Transit van with Death's right hand man at the wheel and your mother's coffin sliding around in the back is less fun than you might think. When Richard suggested it and Gollum – sorry, Callum – agreed, I imagined something like *On the Road*. Instead this could easily turn into the final scene of *The Italian Job*. I've got to say something.

'For fuck's sake Callum, can't you slow down? We've unsecured cargo in the back.'

'You wanted to make good time, Mr White.'

Naturally Richard has to have his say.

'For once I agree with Robin. Mother's woodwork is getting ruined.' *Mother's woodwork? Makes her sound like a carefully restored Morris Traveller.* 'We paid extra for the finish you recommended, remember?'

'So you did, so you did.' Do I detect a smirk on Gollum/Callum's face? 'Brace yourselves.'

Even as he speaks we have to brake suddenly, causing Mother and her woodwork to slam into the wheel arch. He's bloody well enjoying this. Rebecca, on the other hand, is her usual sour self, emitting waves of contempt so powerful I'm surprised they don't block her mobile reception. The only word I've heard her say all day is 'Twat' in response to one of Rich's more pompous remarks.

By now it's one o'clock and we're well south of Glasgow. Balmore's full Scottish breakfast is an increasingly distant memory. I'm getting peckish.

'There's a service station a few miles ahead. How about stopping for lunch? I'm keen to see if the *Welcome Break* lives up to its name.' Mutters of agreement all round, and ten minutes later we're pulling into the car park.

Once inside Becs heads towards KFC. Callum, on the other hand, seems transfixed by the scene before him. Is he staring because he's appalled by the crass commercialism or because he's never seen such sophisticated delights?

Then without a word he strides toward M&S and I meekly follow. Richard has issued Callum with £20 walking around money (or 'per diem expenses' as he insists on calling it) but I'm sure I see Callum surreptitiously slip a tuna and cucumber baguette into the pockets of his capacious jacket. So *that's* what he was doing a moment ago — checking for security cameras. I have a growing admiration for his dark ways.

RICHARD

Long day. And boring. Nauseating to start with as Callum flings the van from side to side and the coffin slides a little, responding to the vehicle's movement. I sit in the back with a pillow behind me and a blanket over me and my feet against the coffin to stop it sliding. There's a smell of flowers that makes me queasy. Callum, for reasons known only to him, has brought plants to sit alongside the walls and in the corners. Orchids look beautiful but they smell foul.

'What are they for, Callum?' I ask. He smiles enigmatically. Does he hear me? Does he choose to ignore me? He focuses on his driving, determined to do it as badly as can be humanly possible. Even Robin complains. Even Robin goes quiet eventually.

It's not so bad once we get on the motorway. This limits even Callum's ability to take bends at speed as the road is straight. Mum's coffin, with its linseed varnish and brass handles, glints softly in the sunlight that sneaks in through the van's limited glassware. I drift off to sleep for a while.

In that strange reception area between being awake and asleep, I ponder the word 'undertaker'. Callum's firm proclaims its status as 'Funeral Directors' and mentions Chapel of Rest and Memorial Masonry but there's not a word about being an undertaker. And, when you think about it, it's a strange word, is it not? The undertaker takes a body under. Under the ground, using a spade to dig a hole, then lowering the coffin into the hole, earth to earth, dust to dust, and it's all so horny-handed. If Mum is cremated – as I want her to be – she won't be taken under ground. So will we take her over ground? Her smoke will rise into the sky, and that seems better to me, perhaps the only comforting thought I've had for days. I'll be her overtaker.

I'm shaken from my reverie by a sudden swerve in the van's direction. 'Good man, Callum,' says Robin. 'Suddenly ravenous. This might be our last chance for a while.'

To be honest, I'm pleased to stop and get the others out of the van. While they go inside the service station I open the back doors of the van – discreetly, of course, I want to protect Mum's privacy, at least until we get to our first destination.

The stop also means I have a chance to ring ahead. I'd looked up Hartley Hall and it's more to my taste than Balmore. Just from the pictures and the website I feel closer to Mum in this place. It seems more her, there's an elegance about its Arts and Crafts style that appeals to mother and son.

A voice answers the phone that surprises me a little. I can't quite place the accent. He introduces himself as 'Cecil Ryan' but the voice and the name don't quite go together. Anyway we have a brief conversation and I tell him that we'd like rooms for the night and the chance of a conversation about my mother. 'Indeed? Who might she be?' He feigns ignorance but I'm not deterred.

Lucky I rang, actually. He doesn't have many rooms and there's only one double, one twin and a single available. I snap them up then realise there are some tricky choices to make about who has what room. I will have the double. I hadn't thought much about Callum before – perhaps he can sleep in the van? Either that or share with Robin, it's his choice. Rebecca must have the single.

I feel in need of something to settle me when the others return. I wash the tablet down with a swig from the water bottle. Pretty soon, as we pull away, I start to feel calmer again. *Perhaps you could be a doctor?* I remember Dad's words, all those years ago. Perhaps he was right after all.

You could be a doctor. Once Dad said it the idea took root. At least in his mind. And in Mum's, I guess, so I wanted to please her. *You're good at looking after people. You're kind, you care.* It sounded good to have people think of me like that. Kind and caring. I wasn't sure it was me but what if what if it could be me me me.

I could be a doctor.

I could have been a poet. I could have been a priest. I could have been a bus driver, I could have been a thief. I could have been a traveller, I could have gone around the world and come back with no expectations put on me except that I might just take off again at any moment just on a whim, a whim of my own making.

It was only ever me he wanted to decide for. With Robin, he didn't give a toss. Robin could do whatever he wanted, as if he didn't belong to us at all. I hear them talking about directions. I could have been asleep.

Where are you? Please don't give me the silent treatment.

iMessage, 22 Mar 2013 11:21

PLEASE

iMessage, 22 Mar 2013 11:26

Rebecca White Q. Can life get weirder than going to Scotland's monument to animal torture to find my dead mum who wasn't even supposed to be there?
A. Yes. Now I'm in a white van with my family, and only dad's missing. That's right – MUM'S IN THE BACK!!! We're taking her to see some of her 'special places'. Swear I'm not making this up. But at least we're not in Scotland any more. We're going to the Lakes, which could be nice, but won't be because mum's dead and my brothers are nut jobs. Wish dad was here.
Posted at 11:37am

Like · Share · Comment

Rebecca White Callum's driving us. He's an undertaker. You can tell by his gay demeanour. That's irony BTW. Hasn't smiled ONCE this whole time. Do they learn this in undertaker school? Can't really see him in another job. He even WALKS like an undertaker, like he's carrying something heavy. And he likes flowers.
Posted at 11:46am

Like · Share · Comment

Not going to text you again until you reply.

iMessage, 22 Mar 2013 11:50

Just had to tell you this. We're in Lakeland! WYWH. Just saw a host of golden daffodils.

iMessage, 22 Mar 2013 13:56

Robin emerged from coma, rambled on for an hour about how concrete housing estates are the only architectural truth in a world of oppression and unemployment or something. S'pose he'd know.

iMessage, 22 Mar 2013 14:35

Can't believe I thought he was a kindred spirit!!! Like him better asleep. Which he mostly is, thank God.

I'm SO PISSED OFF. Dishwater seems to think he's some sort of cultural authority now, and that he actually has the right to TRASH THE LAKELAND POETS. His dazzling analysis: a bunch of pretentious wasters with no conception of real life. Well that's proof to me they had something right.

Not their idea of sibling affection though.

CALLUM

Nobody said a word about detours. Not till we were almost on our way out of Scotland. And then suddenly they're looking at maps and talking about how to reach a hotel on a lake. 'How could we not have known about her trips to the Lake District?' Richard said three times in a row, then he and his brother had a fight over the map, with the result being it tore in two pieces.

I ignored this, so much weirdness, thinking it was some kind of game, a family tradition, like the time-passing things Corey and me used to play at in the car on our trips, in those years after Mum and the old man had just met. Spot the Hearse, or Spot the Ambulance, or Spot the Red Face.

Ignoring the White family's private affairs comes fairly natural. My place on this solemn, long journey is silence. The old man said that, and was adamant. 'Your place is to drive, not to be chatty.' (As if I've ever had a chat in my life.) 'And don't muck it up, son,' he added. It was that 'son' that made me know he was worried.

Nothing bad's going to happen, I think to myself, feeling my foot shake uncontrollably. Headwinds push against the van, making it feel held-back and heavy, like it's carrying a box full of lead instead of just a normal-sized dead woman and three living passengers. Then the wind shifts, gusting from the side. For a second the van is so light and inconsequential that I expect it to lose traction and blow into the sky, joining the clouds. The wind gusts again. I catch myself thinking that somehow the van must be lighter than air, that I – my thin body, in my loose-fitting suit – might be all that's holding it down. My grip on the steering wheel tightens.

'Callum, Callum, Callum,' I hear Robin say. 'Come in Callum. Are you there?' And he makes a sound like space-radio static. I ignore him.

We cross the border, passing from Scotland into England, and the wind dies. The clouds become darker and thicker. Specks of rain start to appear on the windscreen. I look back in the mirror, watching Scotland grow lighter and smaller behind us. *Welcome to the dark side*, I say to myself, not very loudly, and laugh my not-really laugh, but quietly, not intending to be heard outside my own head.

'He's talking to himself over here. I think he might be off on one,' Robin says, as if there's a pane of glass between us, or like he assumes that I'm deaf. 'Will you leave him alone?' Richard says, and I hear Rebecca sigh, maybe because she's already had enough of the confines or maybe because she's read something on her phone that's exasperated her.

For a long time, I drive, thinking about plants, about the orchid next to my feet, whether it needs water or heat, whether the cold air from the air conditioning might be damaging it. Wondering whether it's too cold for the plants in the back, I turn off the air conditioning. Behind me, two brothers bicker like children. I try not to listen. The clouds get even darker. The lines on the road pass under the van.

When my ear goes hot, I wonder if I'm having a seizure. A voice in my ear says 'Callum? Callluuuuuummmmmm.' It's Robin. 'The exit is in two miles, Callum. Did you get that, Callum?'

I look straight ahead, thinking of the old man, of the seizure he'd have if he found out I'd made an unplanned stop in his van. Rebecca says something. I hear the word 'plants'. 'Say it again, Rebecca?' Richard says, and she answers, 'I said Mum liked this place because of the plants.' She's holding up a picture, which Robin grabs from her, slapping it down on the steering wheel. Stealing quick glances at it, a stranger's thin hand on my wrist, I see a large house with big windows. But mainly I see big exotic leaves, a massive glasshouse.

'We're going to this place – you got that, Callum? Can you see the exit?' He presses down firm, applying more pressure than necessary, because the wheel's already turning. I'm turning it.

RICHARD

'Hello!' My voice floats out of the lobby and no one comes back with it. At least the absence of people gives me a chance to look around a bit. The others had sent me in on my own, unwilling to put themselves out at all but pretending to be scared. Pathetic, all their jokes about the Bates Motel. This is nothing like that, it's light and airy despite the wood panelling everywhere. A tall stained glass window of a landscape with green hills and blue water dominate the hallway and the staircase up to the first floor. It's clever because you expect landscapes to be horizontal but this one is vertical, as if pictured from the top of a mountain looking down. *This could be yours* whispers a tempting voice inside your head. Well, it was Mum's. At least that's what the postcard indicates, her favourite for summer.

'So sorry to keep you waiting,' says the rather effete voice that blows in with the breeze through the just-opened front door. Cecil Ryan introduces himself to me, and I explain that the others are waiting outside in the van.

'No *problème*,' he replies in a strangely French accent. 'Please take a seat.'

I ask if the chair's a Rennie Mackintosh, because that's what it looks like. He replies that it could be, and insists that I use it. 'Furniture is not just for admiring. It has a purpose.'

It also has tendrils of vines carved into the high back of the chair and these are not so comfortable, so I lean forward to give him the details he needs. Once I've booked in, he takes me on a little tour through the reception rooms and the conservatory that is bursting with flowers, then out into the grounds. The gardens are particularly beautiful and I feel closer to Mum in this setting. I imagine her on this bench in summertime with the scent of honeysuckle, looking out to the other side of the lake where the mountains change colour as they rise higher. Right now, in spring not summer, there's snow on the mountain tops. It's a good chance to broach the subject, now that I've been polite about his property.

'I think you know my mother. Or rather, you knew her.'

'How was she called?'

'Her name was Iris White. I understand she stayed here, particularly in summertime.'

Ryan looks at me. He pushes back his ridiculously long white hair with his hand, and there's a sudden glint in his eye. He tries to cover up the frisson of surprise when I say Mum's name. When I refer to her in the past tense. When I show a photograph of her.

'There are so many guests over the years. She might have been here, she might have not. It's hard to say. But "Iris White", no, it's not a name I remember.'

I get him to agree to look back over his records, previous years' visitor books. Then he reminds me that the rest of my party have not yet been welcomed to the house. He's right, so I go off to the van to bring them in. I must say I feel a bit ashamed of the bedraggled crew that slouches into the hall behind me.

Rebecca soon disappears to her room. Robin and Callum seem surprisingly relaxed about having to share. 'I don't suppose we'll get in each other's way much,' says Robin. 'We probably won't even see each other.' I arrange to eat dinner later and suggest to our host that we might continue our conversation. 'My pleasure,' he purrs.

But at dinnertime he is occupied with the few other guests. I cannot demand too much without appearing rude, and here I feel rather aware of Mum's presence, as if she's looking down on my behaviour. I'm not comfortable and the only answer is to eat and retreat. 'No sign of Iris White,' he hands me this information with a choice of bread. The river trout sits on a plate with a picture of a fish in bright colours. By comparison the trout looks brown, perhaps browned off, as I slit her sideways to reveal the backbone. The trout's eyes look at me, glinting and black as I lift the flesh off the fishy skeleton and squeeze lemon over it.

I don't believe him but what am I to do? It adds to the mystery of Mum, as if even in death she is still covering her tracks.

A bigger mystery right at this moment is where is everyone else from my family? Rebecca is keeping herself to herself in her room. Callum is in his room but he tells me Robin has gone out. It's all very fishy. I need something to help me sleep.

ROBIN

I'm amazed to think Mother loved this place. According to Richard it's an Arts and Crafts masterpiece and, yes, the reception is very nice if you like that sort of thing – which I don't. It's all very well hankering after a medieval golden age of artisanal excellence but unless you're willing to put up with a bit of bubonic plague in your pastoral idyll then the whole thing is shamelessly synthetic. I wrote a closely argued essay on this very subject during my second year at York, or rather I would have done if I hadn't lost my notes in The Minster (the pub, not the big church).

Still, I'm glad we're here, mainly because I feel the urgent need for a smoke. The sooner the others are tucked up watching Celebrity Masterchef or whatever blows their skirt up, the sooner I can slip away and achieve satisfaction. Unfortunately it's just started pissing down in spectacular Lakeland fashion. Normally I'd take a nonchalant stroll around the grounds and use that as an opportunity to blaze the crop, but walking out in this weather would look distinctly weird, and I can hardly spark up with the other smokers on the covered patio.

Time for Plan B. As Richard is struggling up the stairs with Becca's bag I see my chance.

'Callum, can I have a word? I need the van for an hour or two. We agreed, remember?'

I hold out my hand for the key.

'That we did.' No sign he's about to hand anything over.

'Is there a problem? Because I've places to be and people to see.'

'It's not the van, Mr White, Robin, it's the contents. It's better if you don't take your mother with you. It could get me into some trouble.'

'Well, what do you suggest? We can't exactly sneak a coffin past reception or claim it's an item of novelty luggage.'

'Hmm, let's see what's out the back.' He leads me out of the hotel and round the side to a range of outbuildings. Callum tries several of the glossily painted wooden doors; all locked. Then, just as we're about to give up and get out of the wet, the one nearest the main building clicks open.

'We can leave her here, in here where it's quiet.' Callum suggests as he pulls open the surprisingly heavy door.

I think we were both expecting a nice empty space ideally suited to the temporary storage of dead parents. Instead we're confronted by an Aladdin's cave of exotic foodstuffs racked neatly on shelves and pallets. We glance at each other.

'Really? I mean, isn't it a bit... unhygienic?'

'Ah, well. I mean, who's to know?' I suppose Callum's line of work makes a chap blasé about the dear departed.

Moments later he's expertly backing the van up toward the gaping door while I clear a suitably Mother-sized space amongst the tins of anchovies and jars of sun dried tomatoes. And when you think about it, what's the problem? It's a storeroom, isn't it? All we're doing is a bit of storing. And the sign in the hallway clearly said guests should make full use of *all* facilities.

Soon I'm bumping along a sandy track through a wood about a mile from the hotel. What a lonely place; thank God Mother is stashed amongst tins of chestnut purée back at the hotel and not here to freak me out. I park up, open the driver's side door and listen. Utter silence, except for the rain and an occasional distant car. Perfect. I slam the door and set to work.

CECIL

Mon escritoire. My little *élysée*. It's been too long since I took refuge here, the casement window open, a slight breeze rippling Windermere. In my beautiful house, *mon temple*, has come, uninvited, and so chill, a shadow. It meanders, dulling the polish on the bannisters and the wainscoting, a veil once scented, now free. I cannot smell the beeswax.

It's years since I've felt compelled to write. Your letters still, my once and only, in the pigeonhole. I'd found a calm, by way of the subtle art of suspension. This visitation, though, has jolted me.

How can they be her brood? Yet, it is her. They come to try to understand her. Look, I say, look. She felt all a-shiver here. The beauty of the place is apparent to all but the crassest. The son nods and he dines and he drinks my Pouilly Fumé. He won't like the bill. But those with recent grief have slack wallets.

As he withdraws to the fire, sees the moon on the lake, ascends the stairs to bed and notices the spangled starlight through stained glass he'll sigh, she loved it here, of course. The curtains, the tapestries, the cushions – everything seduces. *Bien sûr*. And the summer nights are balmy and steal away every care with moth-like fairy fingers.

But none of them will understand how she was loved. They won't. They can't. She was their mother.

REBECCA

From: Rebecca White
To: Iris White
Subject: Lonely as a cloud

Hi mum. Well we're in your favourite place for summer. I guess you know this because you're here too. Sort of, anyway. Strange to be emailing you when we're in the same place. Richard's got it into his head that you need to see it one last time. Which I don't really get because you only get to be in the car park. I suppose it's him who needed to see it. We've never really seen eye to eye, but now I don't get him at all... And as for Robin, he's like a total stranger. I've always had this idea of him, based on seeing him for ten minutes every three years or so, but close up I don't recognise him at all. It's like aliens have hijacked his body.

I don't really get any of this as you've probably gathered, but we're here, and it's the longest we've spent together since I can't remember when. Which is good in theory. But in reality it's like a bad film.

So this was one of your favourite places? It's better than the first one anyway. I would have liked to come here together some time. Wordsworth lived just around the corner. But apparently your favourite places are just for you.

So now the million dollar question – did I know you any better than I know Robin? Honestly, I don't have a clue anymore. The thing is, you were always desperate to protect me, which you did by overreacting to everything and shutting me away. Like sending me to Catholic school so I'd be away from H. He's my soulmate, mum, even if he is being a bit of a child at the moment. You just couldn't see beyond your precious social conventions. Well that plan didn't work. But you shut me away from you too, mum. You did better at that. What did you think you were protecting me from???

Their mother was a rare flower. If I'd been more certain... Prepared. Bold. But your shadow is ever with me, and in that shadow the shame and beauty, the remaining question in what for a while was the answer.

What am I thinking though? I was her host. Her summer host, she told me... each summer.

I notice how I slip into the past tense so effortlessly and hate that easy acceptance as if it masks a kind of relief, triumph even. Why would that be? If anything, she gave me a faint sense of hope — not of any greater intimacy between the two of us, but that love and ardour, not just companionship, were possible as nature's silvering takes its course. That what might, by the young and proud, be called decline or disfigurement was more a re-confirmation that evoked desire, a changing map with not only new contours but new paths, both bridle and foot, superseding older rights of way.

She enjoyed her summer love here, with such splendid innocence, framed and couched by Voysey's sympathetic design. It was beautiful, like fireflies and bats in the twilight.

But in the openness of her summer I saw the flower she really was, not of here with its manicured lawns and topiary, but of the untamed meadows of the upper Thames and Magdalen, the delicate puce of frawcup, the snakeshead fritillary, gypsy beauty of Old England's hay meadows.

They can't understand her poetry — late April's flower, although a louche Wordsworth and now I, might evoke April's died-back daffodil, limp after joy, gold in repose. That's how I inadvertently saw her once, sated, curled, feigning dead. He was naked, upright, staring out over the water.

Where is he right now? Does he know?

REBECCA

How long are you planning to keep this up?

iMessage, 22 Mar 2013 22:35

The first time we met in the Lakes, we went night swimming. It was Angus's idea, of course. The water was cold and inky. The stars shone bright, streaking light across the waves. Angus was a silver fish, flicking in and out of the water. Our bodies shook when we kissed — with the cold, with the heat of our mouths. I never wanted to leave.

When I'm with him, I'm brave and bold and beautiful. I do reckless things, wonderful things, things I thought would never happen to a woman, to a mother like me, a (bad) wife like me. He makes me live.

'I want to know every bad and crazy thing you've ever done,' says Angus, kissing my hands.

'I can't,' I say and it's not because I can't tell him my secrets. It's because the wildest thing I ever did just happened. It always happens with him, never before.

'I'll never get used to these stars, my love, no matter how many times we keep coming back,' he says.

My face reflected in the lake's surface doesn't look like mine. Tangled hair and wide eyes.

'I'll never get used to you,' I think, 'I never want to get used to you.'

But I don't say it out loud. I tell him about *Ipomoea*, moon flowers, which only bloom in moonlight. The flowers close when the sunlight touches their petals. That's how I feel when I get home after these trips.

Day 8

SATURDAY

Wherever I am it's dark, cold and incredibly uncomfortable. As I inch upright it all comes back – I'm in the van and the van is in a wood and the wood is in the Lake District. Of course. I should have known my plan for five minute's horizontal rest after the thrill of BBC Radio Cumbria's easy listening hour was a big mistake.

A little later I park the van and saunter up to the ornate front door. My reflection in its coloured glass panels shows one side of my face still embossed with the weave pattern of the van's vinyl seats. Beyond I can see Richard standing by the reception desk, engrossed in a phone call. Judging by his pained expression and the way he's constantly pinching the bridge of his nose while screwing up his face and shaking his head the conversation isn't going too well.

At that moment he looks up, and I beckon him over to the front door while miming unlocking motions. He flips the latch, but just as I'm about to give him some guff about taking an early morning constitutional he turns on his heels and heads back to the phone – clearly not a man looking for conversation. Fine by me. I grab my room key from behind the desk and head upstairs. Rich's replay of whatever drama is unfolding down the phone will sound much better after a couple of hours' decent kip.

I wake early, head crammed full of dreams. They stay packed inside my head, but I can't bring any of them out into the first glimmers of daylight. I feel stuffed, my brain a pustule that needs to be burst.

I hope a shower will do the trick. It doesn't. Perhaps a walk in the garden?

I head that way but my phone rings when I reach the hallway. It's my father on the line. There are no pleasantries to break the ice, straight in there.

'Where are you?' he demands.

'Where am I? Where are you? Are you back in the country?'

'I just got off a plane from Havana. I'm jet-lagged, upset and feel like shit. How about you?'

'All that but not jet-lagged.'

'So, to get back to my original question, where are you?'

I suppose I could have prepared for this. But you sort of expect your own father might be a little bit sympathetic when your mother's died and you've been doing your best. And when you've got his other children in tow, looking after them. Not to mention his wife, my mum, in a coffin in a white van.

'Dad, it's a long story. Not sure I'm ready to go into it all now.'

'Oh, for fuck's sake, Richard. Just tell me where you are!'

At this point I notice someone gesticulating outside the front door, wanting to be let in. To my horror I realise it's Robin. But it's not obvious. He has a wild look about him, like one of Milton's fallen angels just clocking off after a long night stoking the inferno. I let him in, then ignore him as he walks up the stairs.

Dad is still on the line, expecting answers.

'At this moment I'm in the Lake District.'

'The Lake District? May I inquire why? Or will that involve a level of honesty beyond the reach of this family?'

'Just let me say we're on our way home.'

'What, after a long night out? I thought you'd gone to Scotland. Where, for reasons quite beyond me, your mother chose to die.'

'We've been to Scotland, Dad. We're heading home. We have Mum in her coffin. I have everything under control. And I suggest you speak to Julia who's organising things at home and, I dare say, might need a little support from you.'

The rest of the call is a lava flow of incoherent anger. What could I do? I don't suppose he even notices when I press the button to cut him off. Mobile phones are a curse, I hate being on constant call so I turn my mobile off for a while. No doubt I'll have paternal shifting of blame awaiting me on voicemail when I turn it back on.

I suddenly realise that I haven't returned any of Julia's calls. I must ring her when she wakes, before Dad gets to her.

I sit down in the drawing room, feeling terrible, pulled in many directions. I could head straight home, I think, but that would just put me in direct contact with Dad quicker than I'm ready for. On the hall table I see the leather-bound book, with gold blockings of flowers on the cover, and I open it up.

That man Ryan has told me there's no Iris White in the visitors' book, and he's right. But there is some familiar handwriting claiming to be Miranda Tempest, gushing with praise and with an even more effusive message from 'Bill'.

I need breakfast. I sit down to a kipper and vinegary contemplation. The consolation of mastication. Mopping up with a slice of brown bread and bad thoughts. Oh Mum, what the hell were you playing at? What what what what what? And why? Tell me why, tell me, I'm waiting.

CECIL

They're putting their bags in that ghostly van. It's as white as a bathtub. It makes me uneasy. And I'm sure that spectral youth has been rifling in my greenhouse.

They are like 'the lost', *les perdus*. Ultimately we are all in hands as uncertain as these. *Plus ça change, plus c'est la même chose...*

At times like this I cling to my Frenchness. I suppose I could never understand my mother's grace and poetry either, just the lilt of her tongue.

We're back on the road, which is a relief. If any of the White family thinks anything's strange about the three extra plants that we're carrying, that I've propped next to the coffin, they haven't said anything. Flowering specimens, which smell of perfume.

Robin is in the back of the van, talking to her, talking to the box. He smacks it. I want to smack *him*, but instead I draw breath, reminding myself — it's not my mum in there, it's his. 'Can we have some heat back here?' he shouts out. I ignore this at first, but when he says it again, not just once but three times, rapid fire, I turn on the heat. It will be better for the plants anyway.

'Callum,' Richard says, 'we should stop here for fuel. I need a bottle of water.' He doesn't reach for my hand or blow heat into my ear like his brother did earlier, but his voice isn't calm either; there's some heat in it, the same heat that was there when he said, 'Our next stop is in Derbyshire.' I'm going along with all this, like a boy who's been kidnapped. That's what I'll claim if I'm asked. But the real reason is this: I need to find out what's going on here. Who is Iris White? Was she a botanist or wasn't she? I need to open the coffin and look at her, to be sure what she looks like. I look at the road, like a good funeral director. Under my collar, I'm sweating.

My mobile vibrates and plays the Doctor Who theme, my latest ringtone. I know who's ringing — the only person it could be. I reach into my pocket and silence it. In the back, I hear Robin mimicking the theme song, singing it like opera but wordless, a Susan Boyle wannabe who's forgotten how the song goes. Rebecca has her eyes closed, pretending to sleep. She moans. Richard puts his fingers in his ears. When I glance over at him, his face is as red as my stepfather's, or redder.

Before we get back on the road after the petrol, I hear the voicemail. It's the old man, as I'd thought. He says the word 'Callum...' and then nothing for half a minute, forty-five seconds. There's nothing else but breathing, the sound of a radio in the background.

It's terrible back home. I'm used to being in this house on my own, but there's a quality of isolation in it today that is — I can't avoid using the word — deathly. I keep walking from room to room, hardly able to bear going into the rooms that most reflect Iris — her study, the kitchen, our bedroom of course. But in truth, the more I look around, perhaps subconsciously looking for clues, the more it looks like her signature is everywhere.

Each time I come back into the hall, I see my suitcase, sat there like a patient dog. I can't face unpacking. I go back into the kitchen and sit at the breakfast bar. My head feels like a concrete block as it rests in my hands. I'm muzzy with that particular dislocated exhaustion that only jet lag brings with it. I decide I need coffee; perhaps there will be some mild comfort in ritual. The coffee maker is on the cooker. I unscrew the top half, empty the old grounds into the waste disposal, fill it up with Illy from the nearly empty canister, pour water into the bottom half, screw the top half back on, place it on the hob and turn the heat on. Four minutes or so to wait. I return to the bar and sit heavily, listening out for the familiar gurgling.

I mull over the fractious phone call I had with Richard in the taxi back from the airport. Was I spoiling for a fight? On the flight, I had hoped it might be civilised; I even wondered if this might bring us closer together. But I was ill-tempered from the start. What's wrong with me? Oh, what apart from having lost the faithless love of my life in an unexplained death in an inexplicable location that, somewhere deep down, I know can mean only one thing.

At least I learnt something on the call, not that it has helped my mood, to put it mildly. He's in the Lake District, in fact they all are. Of course they are. Where else would they be? He managed to be both truthful and evasive, a specialism of his. The content of the call was so incendiary that I don't remember what he said word for word, but I do remember him saying, early on, 'Just let me say we're on our way home.' Just let me say? Jesus Christ. How did I manage to be a father to such an anally retentive, priggish arse as Richard? But then he casually threw in the information that they had Iris, my deceased wife, in a coffin with them, and irritation turned into incandescent anger. I lost the plot entirely. I've no idea what I said. Just as well. After a while I realised that he'd cut me off. That might be just as well too, but I still deserve answers. I'm going to have to phone Julia, surely she's been told what's going on.

The coffee pot comes to the boil. I pour it into a West Ham mug that Rebecca bought me for my last birthday. Hardly inspired, but I don't expect to be understood by her, albeit we're both going to have to get to know each other properly now. There's only sour milk in the fridge, so I have it black, and instantly scald the inside of my mouth. Shit.

It's early, too early to phone Julia really, but sod it. She's going to have to take some responsibility for marrying Richard. I dial their home number – they're still old-fashioned enough to have a landline. A groggy Julia dutifully takes the call. She may be conventional, but at least she's got some courtesy.

She answers phones.

'Solomon, I'm glad you called. How was the flight? How are you?'

'Shit, in truth. The house is unbearable.'

'You should come here. I mean, I can come and collect you.'

I don't respond to this, which is rude. I've lost my manners. 'Julia, the thing that I'm worried about... Well, I'm worried about lots of things, but I had a huge row with Richard. He told me he was in the Lake District, with Iris's body, and Robin and Rebecca. I'm not even sure I heard it correctly.'

'Oh.'

A silence opens between us. She doesn't know what to say. Or maybe she doesn't know that much. She appears to confirm the latter thought. 'I have to say that I'm not getting very much out of Richard at the moment.' I grind my teeth at the way she's speaking. Richard's infected her with his starchiness. 'But surely the important thing is for you not to be alone.' Back to that. She's trying to mother me. It's her instinct, it's what she does.

I remember to be grateful at last.

'Thank you, Julia. It's a kind offer. But let me think about it. I do need to do a few things here as well. There's a funeral to organise.'

'We'll talk about that later,' mumbles Julia. 'No need to worry.'

The conversation drifts to an embarrassing conclusion. I have an urgent need to be on my own, despite having an urgent need not to be on my own. All these needs, but no idea what I want.

CALLUM

'How many weird hotels can one woman have stayed in?' I say to Rebecca. Both brothers are in the back of the van, with the coffin. Richard keeps sniffling. He might be crying, but it might also be allergies. He seems like the type who would sneeze around plants. Robin is out cold, in the corner, asleep.

Rebecca doesn't answer, just keeps tapping the screen of her phone. We drive on.

'Who do you keep chatting with on that phone?' I say, finally.

She sighs and says, 'Who do you think? My mum!' This confuses me. Not the standard confusion – it's not that I think there's an app for actual chats with the dead ones, even the ones who have only recently gone on, just that there might be an app for pretending to do it, like a diary, a place to tap out words that weren't tapped while it was still possible.

'Sorry for the loss,' I say, taking a line out of the old man's vocabulary. I catch myself flattening my upper lip, like he does when he says it.

She puts down her phone. 'Are you as dumb as you look?'

There were girls like Rebecca in my school, even though they were Scottish and didn't have iPhones. Same hairstyle. What I learned was, there's no way to win. You can agree or disagree with them, it makes no real difference. And silence only makes them blow up. Staying away, far away, is the only real answer, but that's hard to do in a van. So I laugh my sinister laugh, the one I would usually only laugh around plants.

'You are truly strange,' Rebecca says.

I laugh the laugh again, louder this time, navigating the van round a roundabout, through traffic. The first few roundabouts that we came to made me jumpy, but now I'm used to it.

'And you have a face that only a mother could love.'

Now Rebecca is laughing a strange laugh. It sounds strange to me anyway. In the back of the van, there's loud sniffling. I hear the wavering sounds of someone – woman or man; in this case, Richard – trying not to give over to tears, a sound that's like background noise in the funerals business.

'My mum's dead,' I say. 'She's been dead for four years.'

It's Rebecca's turn to say that she's sorry for me, but she doesn't.

'Oh God, do you smell that?' she says, twisting her face up. 'Oh God.' She covers her nose with her sleeve.

I don't smell it, and I say so, shaking my head and making a note to spray myself with deodorant as soon as I can.

RICHARD

It's a relief to leave the Lake District and that awful man. Ryan was hiding something. Covering up for my dead mother even though she can hardly withdraw her future custom. But he refused to say anything about Iris White or Miranda Tempest. Or Bill.

Of course, I say nothing to Robin and Rebecca either. Not sure they're ready for the suspicions that are gathering like the snow clouds over the mountains as we make our escape onto the motorway south. The suspicions are mine but I really don't want to be having them. But I see Callum and Rebecca cosying up in the front of the van and I wonder what they're talking about. They seem to be understanding each other a little too well. And Robin's spaced out most of the time in the back of the van with me and the coffin.

He comes awake to ask me about the medical uses of cannabis. We even have a sensible discussion about it. Of course I know why he's interested but that's fair enough. I deal in drugs, I'm a doctor. Robin likes weed. Like Mum, I see the pharmaceutical value of plants. I could write an ode to the poppy. Perhaps Keats already has. I never seem to be first to come up with an idea. This worries me a little as I'd like to be first to know what's happening, even if it's only to keep things quiet.

The phone rings and it's an unknown number.

'Richard? It's David Mackintosh here. Balmore.'

'Mr McIntyre,' I say.

'Tosh,' he replies. 'David Mackintosh.'

'Of course. Of course.'

This man always seems to put me on the wrong foot. Such a short exchange is already turning into an awkward conversation. What does the man want?

Fortunately he gets on with it at last. He tells me that he has Mum's mobile phone and is planning to deliver it. Some guff about 'a matter of honour'. In fact, he says, he's already over the border, and where are we?

I thought we'd got shot of the wretched man so I'm not best pleased at the prospect of seeing him again. But he obviously feels bad — so he damn well should — about his failure to find the phone.

Anyway, I tell him where we're heading and he says he'll be there in a couple of hours. If so, he might just arrive first.

'What's all that about, Rich?' asks Robin.

I tell Callum to pull into the next service station, mainly to give me time to gather my thoughts. I decide there's no way of keeping this to myself, so when we come to a stop I have to tell Robin and Rebecca the truth. 'We'll have Mum's phone soon.' We step outside, with parked cars all around us, the constant roar of the motorway in the background, and Callum hovering just far enough or near enough to hear or not to hear. He pretends to stare into the distance.

I explain to Robin – and Rebecca, even Rebecca, seems to pay attention – that Mum's phone is being returned to us by Mackintosh. 'How much is he asking for it?' asks Robin. I stare. I stare at him with an incomprehension I don't have to fake. Robin passeth all understanding. Whereas Rebecca, to her credit, has a glint in her eye, which might be curiosity but might even be a just-suppressed tear.

It's cold standing in the open, and I head inside for the toilets. I need to take control. *In loco parentis* is the familiar term and I'm in that situation with these two siblings of mine. I could do with a social worker. But I'm in charge and they're relying on me to guide us on our way. So it's about time I rang ahead to our next port of call, this place in Derbyshire that's for autumn, according to Mum.

A man answers the phone who appears to be Indian. I hadn't expected a boutique hotel in the Peak District to be a curry house. His voice is soft and lilting and calls up a memory of Mr Patel whom I'd seen at the surgery last week.

You have diabetes, Mr Patel.

So what do I do about it, doctor?

Eat less, Mr Patel. You've brought your illness on yourself.

His face was blank and puddingy, perhaps he was even a bit angry. No point getting angry with me, you've only yourself to blame. You could have been slim and healthy, not obese and sick.

I realise that I'm missing what the Indian man on the phone is saying.

I need to concentrate on his words, not those of my remembered patient. He tells me his name is Adarsh and wants to take a booking for lunch. I look at my watch and calculate that, yes, we will be there for a late lunch. But I mention why we're coming and say we'd like to speak to him.

'But who do you say has died?'

'My mother. Her name's Iris White. Or at least it was.'

The line is crackly and Adarsh doesn't say much. We can carry on the conversation later. He promises a delicious lunch.

So I have this picture of Adarsh in my mind and I colour the picture with Mr Patel's diabetic grossness. This is not what I wanted when I decided to visit these places to get closer to Mum. I feel as if I'm picking up diseases as I go. There's time to take a little something to counter the sick thoughts inside my head, and luckily I have my bag with me.

Rebecca White Derbyshire. Goodbye Wordsworth, hello Mr Darcy. But not the Colin Firth version – the one in the book is much better looking.
Posted at 11:03am

Like · Share · Comment

133

So here I am in the Peak District. It's late morning and I've been driving since five am. The sun came up as I sailed over Carter Bar and plunged down into the pine-thick darkness of Kielder Forest, then on down the Great North Road. Not the most direct of routes, but sometimes it feels important to escape the tyranny of the motorway, to sacrifice convenience for landscape. I kept myself awake with a thermos of milky coffee and thoughts of the Jacobite army in 1745. They got to Derby and then lost their nerve. Charles wanted to march on London, but his advisers were faint hearts. His famous retort to them was, 'You ruin, abandon and betray me if you do not march on.' Who knows what would have happened if he'd prevailed. On such moments our lives and history turn.

I'm here to deliver the phone to the Whites. After all that had happened at Balmore I had little choice, I realised last night as I sat, dram in hand, contemplating the 750-mile round trip. Janet found the phone in the elephant foot waste-paper basket in the corridor outside Iris's room. It's an utter mystery. She was close to tears when I questioned her about it. At least we have it back. How it came to be there is beyond me. Who throws a phone away? Lachlan by accident? Simpson having a senior moment? I'm looking at it now. Pink and floral and still almost fully charged. I can see she has messages. A good friend might be tempted to delete them. Instead, I pick it up, thrust it into my jacket pocket and enter the hotel lobby.

The manager seats me in the restaurant and brings me a strong coffee. The hotel is distressingly chic and neat. Everything is finished in pastel colours, there are fresh flowers on the tables and a *menu de degustation* with outlandish, faintly Eastern-styled dishes made with 'locally sourced' ingredients. I'm reminded just how shabby Balmore can seem. No terriers on blankets here, or old stag's heads needing to be sprayed against moths and larder beetles. I can't quite imagine Iris and Angus spreading out here in the way they did back at home.

It's then that I meet the chef, a small, bright-eyed Indian man, immaculately turned out in chef's whites. He asks me why I'm here and I tell him the whole sad story of the past week. I'm not quite sure what made me unburden myself in this way, but the more I tell him, the more shocked he looks.

'You are sure this lady was called Iris,' he says. 'Not Miranda?'

'Actually, she always booked under the name Miranda,' I said, slightly regretting my openness. It had already been a long morning.

The chef's eyes welled. 'And her husband, it was Mr Bill?'

'Yes, I say,' deciding not to make any more of it than I have to, 'her partner was called Bill.'

He sits down, holds his head and sighs loudly.

'How can this be? She was one of my most special customers. She had become a friend and sister to me. She was not old, never sick. This is not right.'

'She had a heart condition none of us knew about. She didn't suffer, apparently. And, yes, she was dear to me, too. It is terribly sad.'

His public outpouring of grief is beginning to make me feel uncomfortable, so I try to change the subject.

'Her family is on the way. I've arranged to give her mobile phone to them. Somehow it got left behind in all the fuss.'

'I am confused,' he says. 'She never mentioned her family.'

'No,' I said, 'But she was a very private person. And people are different on holiday.'

I can see he is close to weeping and feel something close to pity.

'I'd love to see your kitchen. It's quite a menu.'

With this he perks up and we go through into the neatest kitchen I've ever seen. There are gleaming banks of spices and condiments, many of them unfamiliar to me. I confess to him that I've never much liked Indian food, that I find the heat rather unsubtle. He becomes quite animated.

'It is the Europeans who introduced chili to India,' he tells me, 'and Indian cooks in this country have fallen into bad habits, putting the chili powder in late to make sure the dish is hot. Real Indian food blends flavours: the sweetness of fenugreek, the warmth of cardamom, the bite of pepper and the sour tang of the vinegar. Then the heat is deep and gentle, not harsh and in the front of your mouth.'

His eyes shine as he talks and I feel a sudden affection for him. His life cannot be easy, miles from home, cooking for a succession of sullen and gastronomically ignorant English couples. I know how that feels, right enough. He offers me lunch and I politely decline, but we exchange numbers and I tell him if he ever fancies practising his skills on Highland game, he'd be most welcome.

Not long afterwards I hand the phone over to Richard White, who is as awkward and charmless as ever. They roll into the hotel car park in a ramshackle van of Cattanach's, driven by his rather gormless-looking stepson. Presumably they have Iris's coffin in the back and I can't help feeling a pang, that this halting, faintly disturbing exchange will be the last time I'll have anything to do with her. Lord knows when this caravan of misfits will get back to London, but they have her phone now.

They have her phone and, in the end, I deleted nothing. Maybe it will teach them something. Her secrets are their responsibility now.

As I start the long drive home I think about what poor Angus will do with his life, whether I'll even see him again at Balmore without her. And I curse him for his weakness. He should have been braver. And Iris, too. Sometimes we need to act on our courage.

The afternoon sun beats down on the winding Derbyshire road.

'You ruin, abandon and betray me if you do not march on.'

I cannot work. In India we would be cooking for days. We would be mourning so that the whole town knew. We would be at mosque and in temple. We would bury her quick, honour the life and the death as God sees fit. Not this attitude. The lady deserved better. Do they not love her?

Khadija my wife is hearing all the talking. 'Not near the guests,' she says.

'The lady was a regular visitor with Mr Bill like clockwork,' I was saying.

It is not the Scotchman who asks the doctor-son where is Mr Bill. It is me, ignorant fool foreigner, Adarsh not from the United Kingdom. I do not precisely ask where is Mr Bill, I offer condolences to him also.

She is like my friend, my lady, she walks in big steps across the heather and laughs with all her heart like a woman who has no vanities.

She very much appreciates my work. It is a kind of fusion, but it's not some kind of crazy. She is not one of those emperor's-new-clothes ladies who wants a seafood cappuccino because that is the latest fad. She is down to earth and she has taste and she has a love of Nature. She always asks me this special request: can we forage together when the restaurant is closed? It is my pleasure. I am beginning to know the English countryside but my lady knows all the plants — precisely which fungi are delicious in taste or in texture, which are poisonous to make you sick, which are fatal.

It's immediately the thought in my mind: she has chosen the wrong fungus this time, and God who has made all of Nature has welcomed her into His loving arms. But the Scotchman is saying it is a heart attack. Broken heart, I might be thinking, because she did not ever come here alone, it was always with that man she loves so much, her husband who arrives late, I call him Mr Bill because he always pays it. I cannot think.

The lady's doctor-son does not like me to offer my condolences to Mr Bill.

Every night I ask God in Heaven to forgive my father for his disappointment in me. I am not a doctor. My father wants me to be a doctor like this doctor-son, but instead I am the chef, which is not a proper profession to him, it's what a servant does, a servant does the cooking, but I am looking at this doctor-son and thinking he is looking very unhappy in all his ways beyond the mourning, but I Adarsh, husband of Khadija, I am not a doctor and I am happy. God will give my father to understand this one day, I trust in God, and God will give us children if He wishes it, and I will not force my future son to be a doctor or a lawyer, because I am happy.

My lady of the herbs, she is the one who knows the field flowers that taste like pepper or toffee that is burnt, my lady of the fungi, the hedge-berry, the borage and mallow and wort, the spicy grass, my foraging lady Miranda is dead, and her husband of the condolences I am sending is not her husband. I cannot think.

I'm feeling a little light-headed as I'd snoozed for an hour or so. I have a crick in my neck from sleeping upright in the van. And it's not a happy first sight to have Robin's face close to mine and shaking me awake with his hands on both my cheeks.

'Are we there?' I ask.

'We are. But I'm not sure where "there" has been for you, Rich.'

I blame myself for not being *compos mentis*. Whatever that might mean, particularly in the circumstances. I must resist the temptation to beat myself up for just briefly lightening the heavy load I'm carrying. No load heavier than Robin.

Unless it's Mackintosh. As I stepped from the van, before we could even go inside, there he was greeting us. Even here he couldn't stop being the host. But he wasn't too keen to hang around, or so it seemed, because he's almost combining hello and goodbye with the handing over of Mum's phone. I recognised it immediately. For a woman of such impeccable taste, I'm still puzzled that she should have owned such an object in lurid pink with patterns of flowers. Just one more thing for the growing list of puzzling things about Mum.

Mackintosh departs in a hurry and now we're greeted by a lithe little Indian who introduces himself as Adarsh. Not Mr Patel, I see. He shows us into the dining room, explaining that we might be the only guests for lunch.

'People do not like to go out when weather is closing in,' he says. 'But I am very happy to prepare meals for you.'

I try to say that we're more interested in finding out about my mother than his food. But he's bustling about, seating us at a table, pouring water, showing the menu. I feel like screaming *Stop!* but I look at Robin and Rebecca, and they seem more calm and relaxed than they've been so far. The prospect of food seems to have cheered them up.

Or perhaps it's the absence of Callum? 'Where is the boy?' Robin tells me he wanted to explore the garden.

I sit there frustrated by the fleeting presence of Adarsh. Is he cooking the meal *and* serving it? I'm sure it's delicious but I find it all a little strange. There's fish, local he says, but it tastes fresh from the Bay of

Bengal. Perhaps strangest of all is that Robin and Rebecca are tucking in with every sign of enjoyment. I find it a little distasteful to take pleasure when Mum's body is outside and her possibly incriminating mobile phone is bulging like a tumour against my thigh.

I show Adarsh the photograph of Mum.

'Delightful lady Miranda is always visiting when the wild berries and the mushrooms are best to be gathered. My condolences also to Mr Bill.' Robin lets out a wolf-like howl, half surprise, half triumph. He chuckles 'Miranda' to himself. Rebecca smirks and drinks some water to hide the smirk. But I see it.

Then chef's off again, as if he's avoiding us. A woman appears – is this the hidden sous-chef? – to ask if we'd like tea or coffee.

I can't think. I hate what I'm trying not to think about. There is all this Miranda mixing in with cardamom cinnamon chilli and Bill who's Bill I really don't don't want to know but wild strawberries foraged in woods hand in hand with a pink mobile and the shadow of a man who walks alongside in golden autumn sunshine. And a bed. A double bed.

I rub my eyes. I want to scrub up, wash away these thoughts. I'm in a sudden panic to get away but Robin is luxuriating in self-justification and jasmine tea. The bastard, the absolute bastard.

CALLUM

Who is this Iris White? I say in my sinister voice, laughing my usual laugh. The van is locked up, parked out of view, near the service entrance. I'm having some time to myself in the hotel's grounds, trying to think, trying to step back from this urge that I have, which is to open the coffin, just to see her again, just to check.

Who is this unknown, mysterious woman? I say, getting a mouthful of wind.

A bird squats on a stone column, its feathers ruffled and rising. Wind whips my face and my clothes, flaps at a suit that doesn't fit me at all because it's not really mine – wasn't bought for me, anyway – and the thought that I have is: who is anybody?

I sniff my skin. It smells like skin. I sniff it again and am less certain, of anything. I walk for a while, passing dead summer plants that sway like tumbleweed props in a movie, but stuck in one place.

Next to an old wooden door, there's a bench. I sit down on it, out of the wind, and take out my deodorant, the same brand that I've used since we moved up to Scotland: Sure Men. I spray myself with it, and not only my armpits. It smells like life, I think, like being alive. Not like springtime or summer, like all of the seasons combined.

The door beside me opens. I try to hide my deodorant, but it's too late. Robin walks out. 'Callum, my boy,' he says. 'What are you doing out here?' He seems more alive than he has for a while – a lot more alive. As the door closes, I get a glimpse inside the shed, which is full of gardening tools and darkness.

'Are you sniffing something out here, without me?' he says.

I look down at the ground, my skin feeling hot. He grabs the deodorant can from my hand and looks at it, holds it up to his nose. 'What does it do?'

'It makes you feel fresh,' I say, still keeping my eyes on the ground, on grass that seems green and unseasonal.

Robin puts his hand on my shoulder, gives back my deodorant. 'I like you, boy-undertaker,' he says and starts walking away, almost jogging, a real spring in his step. 'You could be more of a rebel than I am,' he says without looking back.

My mobile vibrates, and I answer it — but don't say anything. It's the old man. I hear the word 'Callum...' There's no radio on in the background.

'Callum's not here,' I say, in my sinister voice. I hold the phone up in the air, reaching for wind, thinking: Talk to the clouds, old man. Talk to the clouds. They're English, like I am.

ROBIN

Richard has always been a bit like Manchester – wet and with strange ways – but since his conversation with Adarsh he's becoming distinctly distracted. Not five minutes ago he was telling me Mum 'wasn't the woman I thought I knew'. No shit. How can someone whose work takes him to the sharp end of life on a daily basis be so naïve? I reckon we're all liars one way or another. And do we really want it any other way? It's our little deceptions that keep the world turning. So I gave Adarsh Mother's photo to keep it turning a bit more.

The last thing I want to do is relieve Rich of command – mainly because I'm allergic to responsibility, I can't begin to match the way he's bank-rolled our expedition and I haven't a clue what to do next – but someone is going to have to chivvy us along. We've come this far and I want to know what Mother was doing and who she was doing it with. Perhaps Oxford will give us some answers.

IRIS

Autumn here. Chestnuts splitting their shells, the woodlands blazing with colour, a wide blue sky, Angus's warm body tangling the sheets. I will never forget his face in this place. I think that I never want to go home. And then I remember the smell of the children's necks and I know that I must.

I cannot work. The lady is in a rough box in a white van in the middle of the roads. All her people, but not her husband Mr Bill, where is Mr Bill, her people are inside crowded worse than a poor family in a slum hut, they do not sleep in beds, they must be some kind of crazy. The field mouse screams when the owl dives to take it, but I am used to that sound.

The lady's doctor-son was always the one who is talking. Not the sick son. Not the girl with blackstorm eyes who is always staring at her mobile phone like a mirror.

Miranda was here but it is spring, there are no fungi for her to pick, she has left this life, she has passed into another life. May God care for her soul like a flower taken out of its earth.

The fields and hedges are not in bloom because the season is late, at least one month, one month late or two, everything out of kilter, and the insects are unborn, and the tiny birds go hungry.

Is my lady some kind of meat? The men who deliver the goods or the linens drive this very same kind of white van, isn't it. The cold air like refrigeration will preserve her body, may God forgive me for these thoughts. My striding botanist lady Miranda is in a rough box not fit for beggars in a goods van with all her people, but where is Mr Bill?

The field mouse screams when the owl dives to take it. Possibly it is the same mouse. Possibly it is another mouse, another owl.

Today her family is showing me that old photograph. I remember Miranda took the photo twice because first time she was talking and saying this one place is her favourite place in God's world and autumn is not 100 per cent autumn unless she is here and we are foraging in the fields together, and she was so happy when she was talking that the camera shook and ruined the photo. So she took the photograph twice. She visited every autumn, regular like clockwork. And Mr Bill.

I cannot rest. His name is not Mr Bill and I am sending condolences by the sad-doctor-son and the sick son and the blackstorm daughter to the father who is not Mr Bill.

And the sick son was seizing the photo all of a sudden, and giving it to me, he said he knew that I would like to keep it, and I was just in that moment ready to decline, but then I thought: Miranda was my first friend in England when I came here and nobody else was taking a photograph of me and this is the one keepsake I will have of her forever, although it is an image of me, and if I was a doctor, and if she was my mother, I would not have her lying like that in a beggar's box. I cannot rest. And I know Miranda cannot rest.

REBECCA

Honestly, whats with you? Cut this crap out please cos I've got something to tell you.

iMessage, 23 Mar 2013 17:06

Just been going through mums phone. Youre not gonna believe this. So GET BACK TO ME.

iMessage, 23 Mar 2013 17:10

SOLOMON

Hours after the call to Julia, and all that's happened is that the kitchen looks like a teenager's party scene. I've resorted to eating food from the freezer that I assume is there for Rebecca's benefit. There's a pizza box, with half the pizza uneaten, and some hash browns, similarly abandoned. I appear to be craving carbs, but disgusted by them too. The only things I've fully dispatched are two bottles of Peroni.

Where in the name of all that's holy and infamous are my ridiculous progeny now? The Dales? Morecambe Bay? Perhaps they should take Iris to Jodrell Bank on the trip south. She always liked astronomy in addition to botany. It would be a nice touch.

I wonder if I should report them to the police. There might even be some vicious pleasure in it. Is it legal, what they're doing? In this era of multiple health and safety regulations, there must be laws against corpses going on a tour of the country, taking in beauty spots and popular holiday destinations. You certainly don't see them being actively catered for: 'adults, £10, children, £5, concessions, OAPs and corpses, free of charge'.

In fact, now I think of it, is that what's happening? Are they having a holiday together? Is this some bizarre kind of sibling bonding vacation?

I try and take my mind in hand. I may be going insane, but then, so might they. Perhaps without Iris around, we're all becoming unhinged. I fish my phone out of my trouser pocket, brushing a bit of congealed pepperoni onto the floor. I notice that it's not alone. My eyes flick up to the worktop again. It occurs to me that I have no idea when Claudia is next due to come and clean the house, or even how to get in touch with her. So much I've taken for granted.

I search for my contacts, short-cutting to my favourites. Angus is at the top. I wonder if I'll be up to playing squash? And of course, he'll need to be told, along with so many other friends, colleagues and acquaintances. The conversations will be impossible. I want everyone to find out by word of mouth, and then maybe send me a card. Let's be English about this. Least said, soonest mended. Bollocks of course, but who needs those conversations? Appalling all round.

And there, on the screen, is Iris's name. With a shudder I realise I'm going to have to delete it at some point. When? Now is out of the question. It's admitting that she's gone. It's also disrespectful. All the things you never think about. The thought leaps into my mind that Iris is gone but Castro is still alive. Castro, whose death I have been actively expecting for about fifteen years, hanging on in there, and yet Iris, who seemed all but immortal, is dead.

I shiver and scroll further down to the Rs. All the reprobate Rs are there together, the scheming bunch. I consider phoning each one in turn, but can't do it. The call earlier was too dreadful, and I can see myself repeating it. I send them a group text instead. I have to rewrite it about six times, because with each version I'm unable to strip out acid sarcasm. Eventually I hope it's got a reasonably emollient tone. 'Hello all. I'm back in the house. It's very lonely. Can you advise when you'll be back? I need to arrange the cremation. Love, Dad.'

I'm not holding my breath for a reply. Instead I go round the house again. Iris always had cut flowers everywhere, but they're all looking tired and sad, and in some cases, simply dead, so I collect them up to put onto the compost heap. In our bedroom, I realise with a jolt that the dead flowers are irises. Too poignant. I leave them where they are.

IRIS

I am the woman with three names — Barbara, Iris and Miranda. I am the woman with three lives — Solomon's disappointed wife, Richard, Robin and Rebecca's exhausted mother, Angus's (or should I say, Bill's) reckless lover. I am the woman with three loves — Solomon's faded detachment, the children's sticky-fingered dependence and Angus's fevered promise and hope.

At home, I become one of those women with a smiling face and sad eyes. I see others like me in the playground. There's a flicker of recognition but we never speak. There's too much to say, too much to lose, too much to regret. It's best left unspoken. We mustn't be brave.

'Anyone for a bevvy?'

Callum produces some cans of Tennent's Super from his holdall. Where on earth did he get them? Not that I'm complaining — unlike His Holiness Brother Richard.

'Er, I'm not sure, I mean really, we've a long way to go and the weather...' I crack one open and swig its sickly contents.

'For fuck's sake lighten up. We deserve it. Callum'll get us to Oxford on time, won't you?'

Our resident undertaker raises his bruise-blue can in agreement. We are brothers of the bevvy.

I belch in fraternal acknowledgement. 'Becs?'

'You're kidding, aren't you? I'm not touching that tramp piss.'

'Just a drop — look, that's not going to hurt.' I carefully pour about an inch into a plastic cup and hold it under her nose. To my amazement she accepts. I suppose when you're fifteen you're up for anything. I certainly was.

Rebecca sips then recoils, shivering and shaking her head.

'God that's *horrible*.'

A car speeds past, then another. Becs smacks her lips a few times.

'Actually, er, once you get the taste it's not too bad. What the hell. Top me up eh, Callum?' She's actually smiling.

We're sitting in a layby somewhere east of Buxton. The day started normally enough with the usual disagreements between Richard and myself about everything from the timing of toilet breaks to the meaning of life. Just as we were about to leave I noticed Adarsh slipping Rebecca a carefully wrapped bundle and hoped it might be food. And yes, now we've stopped for supper it seems he's done us proud.

So here we are, using Mother's coffin as an improvised table for our improvised picnic. What's amazing is that Richard hasn't objected to this display of filial disrespect. I suppose we've been stuck in here with her for so long she's become part of the furniture. All the same...

'I don't want to be around when Dad hears about this,' mumbles Becca through a mouthful of artisanal bread and smoked goats' cheese.

'Hears about what?' I answer, 'There's nothing strange about any of this.'

A second's silence, then we all explode into laughter. It's the first joke we've shared, well, the first that hasn't involved taking the piss out of Richard. Don't tell me we're actually bonding. Outside the iron sky threatens snow, but inside all is warm and jolly. It can't last, and sure enough Richard is soon goading poor Callum into action.

'Well that was very nice, very nice indeed, but I really think we should be making tracks. Just look at the snow.'

'Yes, yes, well, you might be right.' Callum attempts to stand in the cramped space but instead falls forward into Becs who squeals and shoves him away into Richard's lap.

'I'm good, I'm good, no worries.' He struggles upright. It's pretty obvious he's not good and we've plenty of worries. Perhaps I should offer to help?

'Hey Callum, Callum, lemme drive. You sit yourself down, you take a rest. I'll get us there.'

But no, too late. Callum has already clambered into the front and is fastening his seatbelt with ostentatious care. 'No, no, Mr White, Robin, it's all under control.'

As proof he starts the engine while it's still in gear and we lurch forward and stall. Richard – who only sipped his single can like some born-again vestal virgin – is clearly rattled.

'Wait, wait! I really think I should drive. I'm sure I'm under the limit.' He's about to get into the front when Callum successfully achieves ignition and the engine roars into life. He grinds into gear and we're off, throwing Richard back onto Mother's coffin while Becca giggles in a way that suggests she may finally be enjoying herself – that or she's drunk. Either way it's a change for the better.

1. **Richard**
a) called, amazingly got through.
b) told me everything was fine…
c) lied to me: told me that they were in Peak District (no explanation) and there was light snow. I checked the BBC Weather and there's a blizzard up there! So now I can add 'deceitful' to 'distant'.
d) heard giggling and music in the background. Could be Rebecca, couldn't work out the other voice.
e) told him about Iris's committal arrangements. He clearly had no idea about what she wanted.

2. **Rebecca**
a) being a Facebook friend has at least some advantages if you want to know what's going on.

3. **Solomon**
a) have no idea what is going on in his head but I have reminded him I am here to help.

4. Kids

a) called and told them I had spoken to Daddy and he had sent them his love, which, of course, he had neglected to do.

b) will they know or care as little about me as Richard did about Iris?

5. Work

a) everything that Richard is not.

b) slipped away for Branding Science reunion — consolation prize.

c) I should get out more.

d) And cry.

Rebecca can hardly contain her giggles. Robin is on his fourth beer and I'm on my second because I don't want to appear standoffish. Callum has a stupid grin on his face and an excess of alcohol in his bloodstream. We didn't get far as the snow got so heavy, and the beers came out. Lots of them. Even if the weather let us, he couldn't drive on now. He's pulled into this layby after a short sliding drive through the snow. This is our home for the night.

I look outside. In fact I step outside for a few seconds. The van is white but it looks filthy in this pure white blizzard. All the world is white, you can't make out any features, there's nothing to see but whiteness.

'All white outside and all Whites inside,' I joke as I climb back into the van.

No one laughs. No one seems to hear. Robin and Rebecca are chuckling to themselves as they play some of Mum's favourite music on her pink phone.

In the midst of this madness, my phone goes. It's Julia. My only thought is – don't get her worried.

'Everything's fine, Julia. Yes, we're heading to Oxford. Stella next, tomorrow probably as we're staying here the night. It's snowing a bit. A little heavy, don't want to drive in it, but everything's fine.'

She tells me that the arrangements are all made for the funeral. It'll be on Wednesday at the local crematorium. She insists Mum told her she wanted a Christian service, not humanist. I don't feel I can argue any more – anyway it makes things simpler. What do I know about my mother? She's a mystery to me. So I text Dad and send him on to Julia for the funeral details.

I have another beer. Then another. Callum's supply seems inexhaustible and at least it makes me feel a little warmer. As, inevitably, we step outside in turns to relieve ourselves in the piled up snow, the blast of cold air fills the dark van. Returning, shivering, I open my bag and take out a tablet or two to help me sleep. It's going to be a long night in this van.

As I take another beer can to my lips I think of all the things I could have been. I could have been anything but what I am and what I am is what I most want not to be which is the only thought in my head as my eyes close on the revolving darkness and I remember that strange meal served earlier by Adarsh with spicy fish.

REBECCA

All right Im just gonna say it. MUM WAS HAVING AN AFFAIR.

iMessage, 23 Mar 2013 23:35

Day 9

SUNDAY

CALLUM

It comes back to me gradually, my eyes still closed. Snow falling in head-lights, tyres sliding, losing all traction. And me feeling drunk, feeling gid-dy, a strange loss of control, my hands gripping the steering wheel, but not really wanting to either.

I'm sitting up, my head resting against the side of the van, where I've slept. Someone's breathing, raspy long breaths. I open my eyes. It's Richard, his mouth open, his chin resting in a weird position. I yawn, and that's when I smell it, this stench. It's not like the worst of the smells that I've smelt in the morgue, like what came out of the cavities of the old lady who sat at her kitchen table for a week and a half, dead, before anyone found her. No, this is worse – sweeter, more rotten. I sniff my skin; thank God it's not that.

The van shakes, from a wind gust, or from the backdraft of a lorry that's passing. I sit where I am for a couple of minutes, breathing shallow, then open the door and step out.

Cold air stings my skin, but this doesn't bother me, coming from Scotland. What's weird is the scene. It's not the image of England I had – not ugly or crowded. It's something like magic. A lavender sky above whiteness. But the snow isn't deep. The road looks fine and driveable – though there's still a fair bit of snow on the layby, under my feet.

I walk towards the front of the van, seeing shoes, a man's legs. It's Robin, stretched out on a tree stump that he must have dragged here from somewhere. He's out cold. He's been sick.

The van door opens, and Rebecca steps out, stands beside Robin, shaking her head, whispering. 'That's disgusting. And have you smelt what it's like in the van? What is that? What's going on, Callum? Is Mum...' She doesn't finish the rest.

I flatten my lips, trying to activate whatever's left of my dignity – I am the stepson of the funeral director, the appointed driver – and realising there wasn't much dignity there to begin with.

'I don't think I can take any more of this,' she says, her voice wavering.

I raise my hand slowly, emphatic, as if I'm about to say something with undue meaning and depth. I want to tell her, we should just leave. We should get our coats and slip away quietly, into the snow, into the countryside, find a cottage with a fireplace, a cooked breakfast, just me and her.

'Where are we, anyway?' she says. 'We can't be more than a couple of hours from London, can we? What if we hitchhiked? I don't want to be part of this anymore.'

Hitchhiking. It's an idea that I like, mainly because I would never have thought of it. Because now that she's said it, it feels like the finest of lines stands between the idea and it actually happening. A line that's called 'yes'. Birds fly overhead, a skein of wild geese, their V losing its shape then regaining it, perfect. I want to say something that's deep. I want to say yes. And yet – it would mean walking away from my plants, into coldness. Before I can say anything, the van door opens again.

'What's everyone doing outside?' Richard says. 'What time is it? We need to get back on the road soon. Mum wants to see Oxford.'

Rebecca and I look at each other. She kicks Robin's foot, and he moans. The vomit looks to have burned a stream into his shirt, into the snow. 'Time to wake up,' she says, and he blinks into life, slow movements at first.

'Wake up, wake up – our ruler is calling us.'

RICHARD

I could have been a fish

I could I could I could rhymes with good I want to be good wanted to be good
as mum was good but now mum isn't good any more which leaves me where
teetering on the brink of a fall from the mountains in my mind my mind has
mountains they say and they're embroidered with the cloths of heaven.

I wake to the dark cloths of night and light and the half-light. It's no
longer snowing. But there's a storm in my head.

I check my bag, suspiciously open. It's the worst violation, the thief
not even bothering to conceal his contempt by covering the traces of his
robbery. But it's not the first time. I'd noticed some tablets missing earlier
in the trip, but he'd closed my bag before so I didn't know if it was just my
mind playing tricks. Some harder stuff gone now, though; I don't want to
be without morphine.

My first thought is to confront him, then to condemn. But I consider
and change my mind not least because there are three suspects, and the
first suspect is not necessarily the last one or the right one. I can't believe
I was so careless but the beer was the real sneak thief. It robbed me of
my prudence. My dear prudence. Mum loved the Beatles, the song goes
round and round in my head. Out of respect I will keep my counsel, keep
my accusations to myself, and think how to replace the unexpected absence of essential opiates. After all, I'm a doctor still, if not one in perfect
mind but that will pass, as all things must. I just have to get through the
next trial, the next circle of hell, visiting Oxford.

No matter how cynical I get I just can't keep up. If – last week – you'd shaken me awake at four am and demanded to know my opinion of Mother I'd have said she was judgemental, demanding, distracted, cold and so on, before asking why the question couldn't wait until morning. Now it seems I was giving her too much credit. Just as I was starting to feel a little better after my inappropriate physical reaction to Callum's demon drink Becs appeared by my side, phone in hand.

'I've something I think you should see. It's an email – actually a few emails – from Mum.'

'They have the internet on the other side?'

'These are from before. And like I say, you should see them.'

With that she hands me Mother's phone. I manage to focus and yes, the screen does indeed show Iris's inbox.

'Let's see now, hmm, lots of work stuff... lots of domestic bollocks... hold on, that... incredible, not sure I can believe this.'

'See what I mean?' She's unusually serious about something.

'Just look how many points she had on her Nectar Card.' My little joke.

'Oh for fuck's sake, this is serious. Look at the message. *Look at the last message.*'

I scroll to the bottom of the list.

'Can't wait 'til Balmore. I want you. Bill xxx'

Wow. I look up and hold Bec's gaze for a long moment, thinking hard. 'Is it real?'

She shrugs. 'Look at the date on the message.'

Ten days ago, back when Mother was residing in Turnham Green and not the hereafter.

I look at the phone. 'Who's Bill?' The obvious question.

'No idea. I never heard her mention anyone called Bill or William or anything else like that. But whoever he is, it seems Mum and him were... intimate.'

'Weren't they just.'

Bill. So *that's* who she was meeting up in Scotland, and presumably who she met at all the other places we've been. You can't kid a kidder, Iris.

I just *knew* something wasn't right about you. And they say us men lack emotional intelligence.

I walk to the van and find Richard.

'Seen this?'

He reads. He reads again. He looks at me, all questioning eyes and confusion. I speak as he doesn't.

'Yes. Perhaps now you'll believe she wasn't everything you thought she was. In fact let me spell it out. Mother was having an affair, and putting the pieces together from our round Britain odyssey it might have been going on for some time. So all that sermonising she used to torture me with when I'd messed up, well, it was pure hypocrisy, wasn't it? She was a fake, a liar and a cheat. I could hate her right now, but you know what? I can't be fucking bothered. Fuck her, fuck this "Bill" character and fuck Solomon. They deserve each other.'

I don't know whether it's Bec's evidence or my rant but Richard seems to accept Saint Iris's halo has slipped. He disappears into the back of the van looking pretty sick. I expect him to sit there brooding but no; seconds later he bursts forth in the highest of dudgeons.

'Robin, where the hell are my diazepam?'

He's really angry. I didn't know human beings could go that colour.

'You idiot, you could get me struck off. They're dangerous drugs, not sweets. You can't treat my medical kit like, like – *he's struggling for a suitable simile* – some sort of lucky dip assortment placed there for your amusement.'

Ah, sibling strife – just like old times. And the thing I learned in all those far-off fights is that attack is the best form of defence.

'Oh you're damn right I could get you struck off. It's not exactly ethical for doctors to get high on their own supply, is it? The only reason you've noticed your precious pills are gone is because you want one yourself to cope with the news our mother was screwing around.'

I fold my arms and stare him down.

'Yes I nicked your tranqs and swapped them in The Claymore for the weed and what purports to be MDMA. So what? It's not as though you can't get any more. You're a doctor for Christ's sake. Write yourself a prescription if you're that bothered.'

It was wrong, of course it was wrong, but I can't say I care. Oh and yes I did help myself again to his supplies last night — I thought they might still come in handy along the way. Someone might find morphine interesting, apart from him. If I let myself be bothered by every dodgy thing I've done then I'd sink to the centre of the earth under the weight of my conscience. And compared to news of Mother's long-term deception I'd say I look like a saint.

RICHARD

Somehow we manage to get the van out of the layby. A rapid thaw helps. The stomach-churning evidence of our overnight stay — yellow stains on the snow, worse if you look further — will hopefully be sluiced away by the melting ice as the rain splashes down more steadily.

I wish it would do the same for my hangover. There really is no medical cure, certainly not among the asthma and constipation medication that's left in my possession. I see the emptiness of my bag and rage inwardly again. As if things weren't bad enough, Robin manages to make them worse.

He seems unaffected by his nocturnal excesses. You might even call him chipper. He's even done us the honour of changing into clean clothes for our coming visit to Oxford. He won't admit it but he feels the need not to be looked down upon by academia. It's another chip on his shoulder. Really he should look like Richard III.

Now I just want this over and done. Why did I get this idea to visit these places? My mad homage to my mum. With each passing minute my assessment of her changes a little bit more for the worse. But I want to hang on to some good things about her, even if it means ignoring the bad things that are now showing up.

Perhaps it will help to see Stella. I probably know her best of the three of us, but I wouldn't say I know her. You have to respect her academic success; she and Mum were good friends but I guess great rivals too. But plants versus fossils, the living versus the dead. My dead mum seems more on the life side of things. So why should I listen to Stella, whatever she may have to say? How reliable is her story going to be? Can I trust her? Can I trust anyone?

Looking around the van, the immediate answer is obvious. Robin, Rebecca, Callum. No. Do I have to stay with them? For what? Or why, how, when? As soon as we've seen Stella. I call her and give her the news. It doesn't seem a surprise to her, as if she already knows.

REBECCA

> Hey Cal! Its Reb. Trapped in white van. Need to escape. Need a smoke. Any chance???

iMessage, 24 Mar 2013 10:11

STELLA

The programme for next week's conference in Amsterdam has been sitting on my desk for nearly six days now: *The 15th International Paleobotany Conference*. Every time I look at it I feel sick and guilty. Sick because Iris is dead. And guilty because on Tuesday I'm going to be sitting in some brown bar with Jim and Lorna, having a few drinks, talking about our latest research. And Iris will still be dead.

DAY I: 9.00AM ~ MAIN THEATRE:
Palaeozoic gymnosperms, systematics and evolution.

I think it was words like 'gymnosperm' that first drew me towards botany. 'Gymno' means 'naked' or 'bare', and 'sperm' of course means 'seed' – not that most people realise that. Gymnosperms sort of wear their hearts on their sleeves, their seeds on their skin. Conifers and gingkos and ferns – honest plants. Flowering plants are tricksy and cunning. They set up traps and hold their seeds deep inside. But a fern, well, it's open and unfurling and tells the truth.

Iris chose her name. She wanted to be a flower. Bright and perfumed, easy to fall for, full of secrets. Don't get me wrong, I've been happy to keep her secrets, although, truthfully, it wasn't much of a challenge. I hardly ever see the rest of her family now, even Sol – haven't done really properly for years.

So it was awful when he called me. I'm such a terrible liar. I already knew. Angus had got there before him.

DAY I: 11.00AM ~ VAN DER VALK ROOM:
Ferns and lignophytes in Palaeozoic landscapes.

Some time in the Palaeozoic era, lignophytes evolved the ability to produce robust wood, to harden themselves. I like that idea, robust wood. (Of course 'robust' comes from the Latin 'robor', meaning 'timber' or 'tough core'. I love how language makes everything clear.)

This morning on the way back from Plant Sciences, I was struck – as I am increasingly — by how young the students are. How they're practically children. I can't believe that when Iris and I first met we were as young as they are. She was so lively and so, *gorgeous*, that's the word. And I remember thinking that my parents had named me after a star, but that was wrong, that I'd never shine as brightly as Iris.

It was because of Iris that I moved into paleobotany for my doctorate — fossilised plants, hardened memories. I didn't want to be competing with her all the time, wanted to plough my own furrow, as they say. So I specialised in the Palaeozoic Era. 'Ancient life'. Precise and beautiful. Not that the records always are.

I met him first, of course. I knew he was mine because his name (if you shortened it) meant 'sun'. Sun and star. How nauseating. And it's a good thing I never told anyone that, because, later, halfway through the third year, when I was going through that thing with Paul, Iris 'bumped' into him. After that there was a lot of bumping, I suppose. Reader, she married him.

Flowers are always out for themselves, though. They've got no use for the bee once they've made sure he's thick with their pollen.

That sounds bitter. But I didn't exactly blame her. It was almost as if she couldn't help herself. What wouldn't you do if everyone loved you as much as everyone loved Iris?

DAY I: 1.30PM ~ REMBRANDT ROOM:
Reproductive structures of Palaeozoic plants and their spores.

Archaeopteris was the first plant that we'd call a tree. It didn't produce seeds but two types of spores instead. Female-like spores and male-like spores. I love that the females are the megaspores and the males are the microspores.

Nearly two o'clock. They should be here soon. Richard always was a funny boy. Said he'd text me when they were a few miles away. Said something strange about a van, too. I should have told them about the park-and-ride.

He did sound *odd* on the phone. Half apologetic, half pleading. And he didn't really explain why they're coming to see me.

When Iris first asked me if she and Angus could use my flat sometimes, stay over, my first thought was relief – that she was finally going to leave Sol and that this might be my chance. Ridiculous at my age, I know, and potentially enormously complicated.

But I fear that I encouraged them for my own selfish reasons, not out of any generosity of spirit or joy in the happiness of others.

They *were* happy together though. They laughed a lot. They made me laugh. Angus was – is – utterly charming. How could I tell Sol without betraying my oldest friend? He still doesn't know about Angus. Do their children?

Am I still supposed to be keeping secrets?

It's no better being in the house today. I think I may be starting to become agoraphobic. It was too much even to go to the corner shop to get a copy of the *Guardian* this morning. I let the phone ring when I could tell it was Julia. I know I'm risking her turning up on the doorstep, but I'd rather have that than have a repeat of the strained, well-intentioned call we had yesterday.

I've had a text back from Richard, saying that he's got the funeral fully under control and sorted. Has he now? Should I feel relieved, emasculated or terrified by this piece of news? Irritation is a given, but the other emotion is up for grabs. I woke up this morning having no idea how to go about organising a funeral, despite my text to the children yesterday. In theory, it should be good to hear that Richard is claiming to have it sorted. But it's emasculating too. There is no role for me in all this; I'm left to wander around the house in ever decreasing circles, albeit with ever expanding circles of sadness.

I seriously consider organising a separate funeral, a competitor to Richard's funeral. Hey! Why not? It energises me. A Funeral Fringe. Off-Funeral. It would be cool, not like the middle-class nonsense that Richard will have in mind. It would be a big-hearted honouring celebration of Iris's life, conducted outside amongst flowers and plants of all descriptions. I'd get a Cuban Son band in, like the ones she loved to dance to in the early days. We'd all get drunk and laugh, and eat well.

But it's a fantasy, it's not going to happen, so mostly I focus on the fear of Richard's official dirge. Lifeless in every conceivable sense, not just in the literal casket reference. Unless of course he really has lost it, and he has something crazed in mind. And what if Robin has some influence on events? Conducted in some crack den and officiated by his dealer. It doesn't bear thinking about.

Except I can't help thinking about it and imagining it starts to drive me crazy. I need something to do, some distraction. I remember a to-do list I made on the plane coming back, and I go upstairs to retrieve it from the jacket I was wearing then. Most of it looks unbearably complicated, and furthermore is contingent on being able to speak to my children.

I scan further down, looking for something that I can do that would give me the quick satisfaction of crossing something off. And then I see it. Phone Angus. Of course. That's ideal. He's an old friend, one of my oldest, he should hear it from me, and although it won't be easy, it's one of the most approachable things on the list.

It takes a good number of rings for him to pick up; enough time for me to debate whether or not I would leave a message if it went to voicemail. So that when he does answer, I jump in surprise.

'Oh Angus, you're there.'

'Yes, er, hello Solomon. Sorry, I couldn't find my phone.' A pause.

'Anyway, how are you? Are we, um, still on for tomorrow?' There is something oddly equivocal in his tone.

'Well, that's why I was calling.'

'Oh yes? D'you want to postpone? Wait... of course, how stupid of me, you're just back from Havana aren't you. How was it? And your keynote talk? A success, I trust? But forgive me, you must be exhausted. Squash is the last thing you want. We can easily reschedule...'

This is not the measured Angus I know. He's babbling. And I'm getting the very clear sense that something's up with him, as if he would be only too pleased to postpone. Anyway, I need to tell him my news.

'Sadly not, in fact it was a disaster. Wretched. I shouldn't have done it. You see, the day before, or maybe two days before, I got some news.'

There's a long pause now. In a pre-digital age, I'd have heard a crackle on the line. 'Oh?'

'Uh, Angus, the thing is, Iris died. She's dead.' Still nothing coming back from Angus. The silence deepens.

'In Scotland. On some country estate, like a shooting lodge.'

Yet more silence. Then, at last: 'A shooting lodge you say?'

'Angus, did you hear what I said? Iris is dead?'

'Oh, God, yes, I'm just... Solomon, I am so sorry. I don't know what to say. Dead, I mean... Listen, Solomon, this is devastating... for you, I mean. I – I really don't know what to say...' No he doesn't. And now I'm faintly irritated. Angus is the one person who has the smooth manners, the social skills to know exactly what to say in a moment like this. And he's still going. 'Iris. Oh God, Sol – what an appalling thing. Iris? I – I can't believe it. Lovely Iris...' Now there's a tremor in his voice. What on earth's going on? 'Oh Sol, what an utter tragedy – for you. For the children...' His voice trails off.

Ours is a friendship that's been based on weekly squash, laddish banter and beer. We've skimmed well above the deep-and-meaningful, like wispy cirrus clouds making no impact on the earth below. This is alien territory for us both. I try and get back to something more familiar.

'So Angus, sorry, I've lost all track of time, our game is tomorrow?'

'Well yes. But I can't imagine you're up to it, under the, er, present circumstances.'

'Tomorrow?' I look around the room, the walls closing in. 'No, I think it's just what I need.'

'Really? Are you sure?'

'Yes.'

'All right. Well, I'll see you, ah, tomorrow, then.' He has another thought. 'Although presumably the funeral must be soon?'

Where do I start with that one? Too much like hard work. 'It's, it's a long story. I can't get into that now. I'll tell you when I know.'

'I'd want to be there. To support you and the children.'

'Thank you.' I ring off a minute later as the call dribbles to an uneasy conclusion. I decide I need a whisky. As I'm pouring it, something wriggles round in my mind. The oddness of the conversation. His distractedness. His words tumbling out but then all those silences. So very unlike the calm, collected, sometimes even calculating, Angus I've known all these years. Why?

I stare sightlessly out of the window, with a weight like a brick starting to settle in my stomach, accompanied by an almost physical sensation of gears turning in my mind. I down the whisky in one and bring the empty glass down too heavily on the worktop. The glass fractures around the base, and I watch the last dribble of the whisky seep out and drip down onto the floor.

He recited Wordsworth to me. Only Angus, only Angus would spend days trying to find a poem about something that I loved. Wordsworth had written verses on my favourite moorland lichens, the *Cladoniaspecies*.

> *Ah me what lovely tints are these,*
> *Of olive, green, and scarlet bright!*
> *In spikes and branches and in stars,*
> *Green, red, and partly white.*

The next morning while he was still sleeping I wrote the verse in my notebook. No one else could tear open the night like him.

How dangerous it was to live and love this way. How dangerous it was to love Angus, place him in the curve of my longing. And then, the next day return to Solomon and lie stiff in our clean sheets. No one else but Solomon could create such chilling space.

Each time I returned home I carried more loneliness in my arms. But also the lakes, the sound of the leaves underfoot, the smell of earth. And I never lost the smell of Angus's body. The indent of his face on my pillow.

ROBIN

Oxford Uni has 800 years of intellectual excellence; York Uni has the largest plastic-bottomed lake in Europe. Not that I feel inferior or anything.

But what really irks me about this place is the privilege. Just now I walked into the porter's lodge and you'd think I was a minor royal simply because my name was on a list. It was all 'Yes sir, no sir, how brown would you like my tongue sir?' If I really *was* someone of status the obsequious little shit would have grovelled himself to death.

Oxbridge brings out my inner anarchist, although I expect I'd feel differently if I'd got in instead of screwing up my A-levels after that unfortunate misunderstanding over Richard's MG. I'm *sure* he said I could borrow it, and the damage to Nando's front window wasn't anything like as bad as it looked in the local paper. Even the magistrate agreed. Still, probably best I don't dwell on the Dark Times right now; we're on our way to see Mother's friend Stella and I sense we'll need our wits about us.

As directed by the porter we climb a narrow, groaning staircase that terminates in a dark wooden door. Richard knocks and a soft, confident voice bids us enter. Stella – for it is she – rises to greet us.

'I'd like to help you but I'm not really sure I can. Iris and I were best friends of course, but as you know we didn't see each other very often. It was one of those relationships that only came to life when we were together. We certainly didn't chat regularly or gossip about our day-to-day lives. Heaven forbid.'

We've been here ages, passing pleasantries and getting nowhere. Richard seems to accept this while Becca just looks bored. But there's something about this lady that makes me think she's a bit too slick. *What's she holding back?* Let's see if a few tricks from the DC Scrooby school of inquisition work here.

'I can't help admiring your trowel.' Now there's an opening line I haven't used before.

'Really?' Stella turns and looks over her shoulder at a jumble of battered tools piled on the shelves behind her desk. 'I wouldn't have thought...'

'The way it's worn. On the right edge as you hold it. Shows you're left handed – am I right?' Proper little Sherlock today, aren't you Robin?

'Yes, yes I am, how very clever of you to notice!' She liked that. I imagine paleobotanists don't get much opportunity to talk kit with civilians.

'You must have been on quite a few digs with that.'

'I've had it since I was an undergraduate. In fact it was given to me by my tutor who later...'

'What's the best thing you've found with it? I know it's a schoolboyish question but I've a schoolboyish interest in fossils. In fact they've fascinated me since I was small.'

Out of the corner of my eye I can see Richard staring at me in disbelief. Setting fire to his Action Man was more my style back then.

'Oh me too, me too! Well, since I was a school girl obviously.' We share a giggle. 'Now, let me see, gosh, well I was using it when I came across a new species of *Cyatheaceae*, er, that's a scaly tree fern, in Greenland back in the mid-1990s. That was quite a coup. Up until then it was thought they'd first appeared in the Late Jurassic, but my discovery pushed that back by many millions of years.'

'Fascinating, fascinating.' By now I'm leaning forward with my elbow on her desk and my chin cupped in my hand. 'And how did that boost your reputation?'

'I suppose it was a big part of me landing my fellowship here. Before then I was just part of the team, after that I had a little bit of fame.'

'And here you are!' I look around the cramped office in wonder as if it's the interior of the Taj Mahal.

'And here I am!' She appears delighted at my recognition of her achievement.

'Look, I'd love to talk all day but I'm sure you've a thousand things to do. We better leave you in peace.' I stand up, take a couple of steps toward the door then turn.

'Oh, just one thing. It's probably a silly mix up but does the name "Bill" mean anything to you? In the context of Iris I mean?'

She flinches almost imperceptibly. It's nothing but it's everything. Bull's-eye Robin — she is holding something back. 'No, no, I don't think...'

'Only we came across an email to her from this Bill that suggested they were friends. Great friends, if you get me.'

'I...' The other two do the tennis match head turn thing between Stella and me with widening eyes.

'...and of course you knew her better than anyone except Dad, maybe *better* than him. If anyone knows who Bill is, it's you.'

That's it, just let the silence build. Someone has to speak and it won't be me. Come along now Stella, time to tell.

'Well I, um, I might have heard the name.'

'Really. In what context? Balmore House? And the Lakes? And Buxton. And of course Oxford.'

'Er, well, yes, if you must...'

Richard jumps in. 'So you know... everything?'

Big sigh. 'Yes. Iris explained it about, ooh, fifteen years ago.'

Richard again. 'And you've met him? This Bill?'

Pause. 'Yes, yes. Just once. The three of us had dinner together. That's all.'

I return to my chair, polite but chilly. I like her but she did just lie to us.

'You'd better start at the beginning.'

CALLUM

It's Richard's idea that I should stroll in the Botanic Garden. I tell him I should stay with the van, with his mum – flattening my lips, meaning business – and Richard looks at me with a look that makes my spine tingle. It scares me.

'You're going to the Botanic Garden,' he says, grabbing my arm with his fingers, fingers that seem strong for a doctor's. 'Okay?'

And here I stand, in probably the warmest room in Oxford, looking at an orchid with blooms that are more vibrant than any I've laid eyes on before. Purple blossoms – bright purple – with neon orange bits in the middle. The plant stands at just the right height on the table for its blooms, dozens of them, to meet me at eye level. Around it, in six tiny pots, there are six little upstarts with no flowers, but the same sort of leaves, the same potential.

I want one. I lift my knuckle to the main plant, not to touch it for real, only to pretend to be stroking it.

'I wouldn't touch that if I were you,' someone says. I turn around. It's a lad in a gardener's shirt, early twenties, not much older than I am. He's smiling.

'What kind of orchid is this?' I ask.

He laughs, not in an odd way. 'It looks like an orchid, doesn't it. It's not though. It's carnivorous. Eats bugs for its supper. It prefers South American bugs, I'd have thought, but it doesn't complain about the local varieties of Oxfordshire.'

We talk for a while, about gardens and plants – about gardening. He asks if I've ever been to Kew Gardens. I tell him I haven't, but the more he talks about giant lily pads, the contents of the Palm House, the more I remember – I have been there, a long time ago. He's actually worked there, doing the planting. Not to mention the other gardens he's worked in, mostly in Cornwall, which sound, the way he describes them, like kingdoms of quiet.

He asks what I do, and I tell him: a family business. He looks at me as if waiting for me to say something more, but I don't want to. A text message comes through on my phone just as an old lady walks in to the

room, exclaiming and needing to be smiled at and listened to. She guides
the gardener into the next room. The message is from Rebecca.

> At van, traffic warden covering nose n talking on fone about us.
> People r staring. Where are u? x

I look at that x for a long time, knowing without really needing to think
much about it that it's nothing, nothing that means anything, just a slip of
the thumb.

STELLA

New insights into the interpretation of inconsistencies in Palaeozoic plant fossil records.

Palaeobotany, like all studies of the ancient and the long gone, can be a little like feeling around in a bag with a blindfold on. Your fingers can make out the shapes of objects, distinguish between their textures, but your brain struggles to interpret them. Sometimes you get things wrong — you misclassify them, label them incorrectly.

Occasionally, in the fossil record, we find that stages of plant evolution seem to be missing. Or from time to time, we find that a fossil of a plant from a later era appears amongst plants from an earlier time.

But the important thing to remember is this: there is no such thing as an 'inconsistency' in the fossil record. There are only 'apparent inconsistencies'. The challenge for the scientist is to work out what really happened.

So after that most peculiar and exhausting couple of hours, I'm feeling even more guilty and even sicker. Guilty because I fear that some of those secrets were not mine to give away. And sick because I've understood something about Robin.

Robin. I wonder where he learned to smooth talk like that. A flannel merchant, my old dad would have called him. And even though he was rather grubby round the edges, he had the most disarming smile. Utterly charming. Just like his father.

Richard, on the other hand, was very strange. Mind you, he always was rather uptight, even as a little boy. Used to have the most extraordinary tantrums whenever Iris picked Robin up. You wouldn't have thought such a pallid child would have such bite in him.

'Yes, I know Bill,' I said, straight off, when Robin asked me. And once he'd told me that they knew about their mother's affair, it was impossible for me not to tell them everything. Everything, that is, except his real name. Telling the truth is so much easier than lying — you don't have to remember what you made up. I told them how long Iris had been seeing Bill for. I told them how unhappy she'd been with Sol. I told them about how we used to walk across Port Meadow and go to The Trout for lunch. I told them about the cover story they'd invented in case anyone recognised Iris – after all, she was a famous face in our small world.

Robin was amazingly good at wheedling information out of me. He reminded me of those female spies in the war who were able to make the tightest-lipped generals crumple. But Richard sat there the whole time with a glazed look on his face – and then he just left. I don't think he understood a word I was saying. Not a bit like his mother.

DAY 3: 1.00PM ~ REMBRANDT ROOM:
Making sense of temporal patterns in our understanding of the fossil history of gymnosperms.

It's easy to draw false conclusions about how long a type of plant took to develop and diversify because of the variable quality of data available. We have lots of specimens from some time periods, and very few from others. I've got colleagues who specialise in quantitative analysis of the effect this has on our understanding of the tempo of evolution.

Discrepancies are everywhere. We don't like them. We try to make sense of them, to fit them into our preconceived ideas and classifications. I'd never really looked at Robin's hair before, at the set of his chin. I'd never really looked at Robin at all.

It was sweet of him to ask me to the funeral. Of course I would have called Sol to find out anyway. How could I not be there to say goodbye to Iris? She was my dear, dear friend, even if she married the man I loved, even if she used me as camouflage.

I think I owe Angus a call.

RICHARD

I can't stand any more. Robin starts to interrogate Stella as if he's Inspector Morse on a particularly bad day. Rebecca sits grinning like an idiotic Sergeant Lewis. And I can't sit listening to this so I stand up, thinking to myself 'That's my mum you're betraying'.

'Robin, Rebecca,' I say, 'I need air. I need space. Take the van, I'll see you at home, tomorrow probably.'

Robin and Rebecca are so engrossed in Stella's tale, and their own sleuthing, that they don't even acknowledge my words. Did they hear? I might have mumbled. I'm really not feeling at all well. My half-empty bag is no consolation but it's all I have now so I grip it tightly as I walk down the wooden stairs and into the college gardens.

How Mum must have loved this. I look at the ancient chestnut tree and the flowerbeds. Daffodils are everywhere this week. Beyond them are rows of vegetables and herbs under cloches, with greenhouses behind them. There's much here to amuse a botanist, if botany was the amusement of this place.

And why not? Why taint Mum's whole life with suspicion? Because there is always Bill. The name keeps cropping up uninvited – by me at least. I wish he'd go away, I wish he'd never come. I could have been a better son without him.

Without him without Mum without Dad without Robin without Rebecca without Callum without Julia without walls without suspicion without hope without drugs without education without plans without expectations without duties without without...

REBECCA

Rebecca White Just when life can't get any worse, IT DOES.
Now Richard has done a bunk. UNBELIEVABLE. He's meant to
be my SENSIBLE brother. Now it's just Robin the retard and
an undertaker who wants to be a florist.
Posted at 14:03am

Like · Share · Comment

Rebecca White Sorry if I offended any retards.
Posted at 14:05am

Like · Share · Comment

183

From: Rebecca White
To: Iris White
Subject: HELP!!

Mum, we need you. You've always been there when things have gone wrong. But now all the things that need fixing are about you. What am I supposed to think? When I saw those messages from Bill – who is he? – I was like, finally, you don't have the moral high ground any more. Now it's all going round and round in my head. What about Dad? What about us? I just want things to go back to how they were, but they won't will they? And if you hadn't died, would everything just have carried on? Or was it all about to fall apart?

This whole mad trip was Richard's idea. He wants to know more about your life, but I guess you wanted it secret. I thought it was a dumb idea but I kind of respected him for doing it, and dragging all of us into it. But now he's bailed on his own plan. I think he's losing it. I mean, I really think he is. I sometimes call him Dishwater. Well he's not being boring now, but it turns out I miss the old Richard. I miss the old everything.

Once when I was little and I'd been crying, I can't remember why, you held me and comforted me until I fell asleep. I half woke up, and you were still there. You were saying the same thing over and over – 'I'll never leave you. I'll never leave you.' I still remember how safe I felt. But maybe nothing can be forever.

So what now, Mum? Where do we go from here?

IRIS

I knew our marriage was over when I stopped wanting him to be there. He was always absent, but in the early days, I would say stuff to the kids like, what a beautiful night, I wish your Dad was here. But then I stopped feeling it. We didn't need him. We were better as a unit of four. He'd creep into the garden late when the children were already asleep and I couldn't bear to look at him. I'd stare at the poppies on the side of the path instead. They looked like pools of crimson sorrow. Drink? he'd say, pressing a glass of wine into my hand, as if that would make things better.

The first fissure appeared before Richard was born. Solomon had said he wasn't sure about offspring (imagine choosing that word instead of children), he said we didn't have to have them. You should have told me sooner, I said, barely able to get the words out. If this is how you feel, you should have told me sooner. You've never really talked about children before, I thought you didn't want them, he said. Of course I want them, now I was screaming. Of course I want children. I knew in a flash that I would do anything to have them.

That morning I washed my pills down the sink. The following month I was expecting Richard. In nature seeds are spilled but only a few take root. This boy of my mine was determined to be born. I bought three new house plants. The pregnant onion, *Ornithogalum longibracteatum*, the Mexican hat, *Ratibida columnaris* and the spider plant, *Chlorophytum comosum*. They grew scores of baby plants on their leaves that I plucked and repotted and spread all over the house like germs.

I didn't tell Solomon for months. When I was 16 weeks pregnant, he said, You're getting fat. Yes I am. Are you pregnant? Yes I am.

When Richard was six days old, Solomon apologised. I'm sorry, Iris, he said, patting my shoulder with his hand. I didn't reply. It was too late. His words were just words. What was real was this tiny life of mine shuddering in sleep on my chest. I need him in bed with me, I said. It's best if you sleep in the spare room.

For the last hour or so before we reach the White residence, nobody says much. Rebecca takes over the navigating, telling me 'Left here,' and 'Second right on this roundabout,' and such things – her voice even flatter than normal, like a computerised voice, pre-programmed.

The windows are down and the air conditioning is on, which is fine for the smell, as long as we're moving. It's less fine when we stop. There's no denying that Iris is with us, in a way that she'd never have wanted to be, no matter who she really was. I try to focus my nose on the sweet floral smell of the plants that I added in the Lake District, the leafy smell of the others, the daffodil posies that I found by a car park in Oxford.

The van turns on to Iris White's street, a terraced street that seems to stretch halfway back up to Scotland. 'That's it, Number 71,' Robin says, talking rapid. 'The one with the ghastly aqua-green door.'

The van hasn't finished stopping when my passengers step out of it, gasping for air, their bags in their hands. All but one of my passengers, I mean.

'I chose that door colour,' I hear Rebecca say.

'I know,' Robin says. 'Mum hated it, you know. She just didn't want to tell you.'

'No she didn't! How would you know? You weren't even here!'

I leave the van well down the street, so any mourners who come while I'm stopped here shouldn't have to walk past it. I knock with the hand-shaped knocker on the aqua-green door, and wait. No one answers. But Robin, or Rebecca, has left it ajar. So I just walk in.

The back garden at Iris White's house is not what I expect. Paving slabs and white pebbles, a few old mismatching furnishings. A whole part of it is overgrown and uncared for. But there's a glasshouse, bigger than any I've seen on this trip.

As soon as I pull back the big, creaking door, I see things as they are, clear and true. I see that this is who Iris White is. That whatever else she might have done, whatever mysteries, she was the woman who collected these plants and made them stay living. She was the woman who used this trowel to dig holes with, who sat here in this old wooden chair, drinking tea probably, and thinking.

I live with this idea for a warm couple of minutes, feeling a strange kind of comfort, which blooms into a much bigger thought: that Iris White had her life, that it was what it was, whatever it was, and that whatever's out there, outside — in the street, in the van, in that coffin — has about as much as nothing to do with this fact.

At the far end of the glasshouse, I see something interesting. Flecks of purple above a row of various green cacti. On closer inspection, it's just as I thought. It's one of the bug-eating plants like the one I looked at in Oxford. Except that this one is bigger, twice the size of the main specimen that I saw there. This one is covered in buds, four of them open already, with plenty more coming.

On the shelf underneath it, there's a fly, sitting and waiting, easy prey. Come to Daddy, I say to the fly. *Come to Papa.* And I laugh my not really laugh. But the fly doesn't move, sits still as can be, even when I put my nose down beside it.

The door of the glasshouse creaks. 'I knew I'd find you in here, skulking,' Robin says. He looks around, seeming keen to be in here but also uncomfortable, like a foreigner. His face has aged ten years since I met him in Scotland. 'Here's the address of your fellow spookmeister,' he says, 'who'll take over from here with the funeral creepiness. Solomon's written the address down.' He looks at the slip of paper and reads out: 'Funeral Directors, William Parker.' The breath Robin draws in after he's said this is so vast it should empty the air from the glasshouse. 'Will Parker,' he says, already laughing. He laughs so long and so hard that I can't help joining him.

A bald man walks through the garden, frowning, maybe annoyed by the laughter. I can see him through gaps in the plants. He taps on the glass. Robin turns, and the man nods towards the house, a brisk nod like an order, but wordless. He walks off.

Robin clears his throat, speaks quietly. 'Can you help me with something, Callum my boy?'

I nod that I will, and he leads the way to the bottom of the garden, into the weeds and the shrubs, to a shoulder-high wall and a locked gate. 'I used to do this almost every night when I still lived at this house.' He glances back at the house. 'Then one day, I just didn't come back.'

I bend down like he shows me, and he uses my shoulders to step up on, launching himself.

It's only after he's gone that I look at the padlock on the gate and see it's not locked.

Day 10

MONDAY

RICHARD

I can't find my keys. I must have left them somewhere in Oxford but I can't retrace my steps in my memory. My memory needs a little nursing back to health. After my visit to the pharmacy, after the partial replenishment of supplies, I can't remember much. It's like a dream in which a long tunnel stretches out and you just keep moving. Until you stop. Until you wake up properly.

The doorbell chimes, and the look on Julia's face brings me back to reality, to here and now. Is that look horror? Shock? Even relief?

'Richard. Well... come in. You look terrible but I'm not going to ask where you've been. Not yet anyway.'

That, at least, is some kind of relief to me. How do you explain? Mum's behaviour – if you take it at face value – simply cannot be explained. But I have some understanding and, to be frank, I don't believe half of what others might be prepared to believe.

Mum was a good woman. She was a good mother. Nothing else matters to me.

I sit with Julia at the kitchen table drinking a cup of tea. She explains that the children have been staying with her parents. Poor kids. I could love them more. I can't talk, though. The tea, golden brown, has fascinating depths to stare into as I swirl it with my teaspoon.

Julia tells me the arrangements for the funeral. Cremation, as expected. Coffin now with local undertakers, delivered by strange boy from Scotland. Service in two days.

'She was a good woman,' Julia tells me. I know. I could have told you that. 'Rebecca's gone home. Robin's in Robinland.'

I attempt a smile. I probably look like death. The skull beneath the skin peeking through. I've seen enough bodies in my time, and I've seen skeletons, real and plastic. I know how things work. I could have been a mechanic. I always loved playing with Dad's Meccano set. He always let me know it was his. I had to be good to play with it.

'I could do with a bath,' I say. My first words to Julia. 'And a sleep.'

'I'm sure,' says Julia. 'Take your time. No questions for now, let's get the next couple of days out of the way. Then we have to talk. No more lies. But give Iris a good send-off first.'

Oh, I could talk. I could explain that this was all I was trying to do, to give Mum a good send-off. But not now. I can't say anything now.

JULIA

Poor Richard... poor dear fucked-up Richard... whatever am I going to do with you and your fucked-up family... just when I thought I was through, when I had finally seen you for the complete emotional non-entity that you were, seen the father you can't face and who can't face you, for the self-centred fool that Iris must have grown to despise, your whole family for the selfish rag-bag... and I had made up my mind to leave... moving to Branding Science's San Francisco office... you never saw the irony... that I work for a creative medical insights company when I'm married to a medic with no creativity and no insights... you've never known how I was feeling, never known what I was thinking... not the slightest inkling... did you think that when you left after Archie was born and came back that everything would be the same?? Poor Richard. But it wasn't just the job, Richard... there was or there was going to be someone else... there's always someone else, isn't there?... And then you burst into tears... after all I'd tried to get some emotional response out of you... when I squeezed your hand and I thought 'like squeezing blood out of a stone' trying to get you to express yourself... your own mother and not a single bloody tear since she died... and I knew then I was right to go... and suddenly, you were weeping... I don't remember you ever weeping and I'm not sure you even realised it was happening... and when I thought of the rest of them, Solomon, selfish and helpless, Robin, sweet screwed-up Robin, Rebecca, motherless, fatherless, and I thought who's going to hold them all together the way Iris did? So maybe I'm not leaving after all Richard... or maybe you and I, we'll go to San Francisco together.

Or maybe we'll stay as we are... Maybe I won't tell you any of this, Richard. Maybe I will. Maybe I won't. I know I said 'no more lies' but when I think of everyone at the funeral, when I think of holding your hand... I think... maybe it's best if we just carry on, you, me, all of us, lying till we die... maybe...

CALLUM

The glasshouse at Kew Gardens is a monster, bigger even than what the gardener in Oxford described. Not that I should have needed to hear it from him. One look over the old metal viewing platform and I remember it all. Me and my mum, a Sunday. She saw how excited I was here, and she encouraged me, hugging me, reading the labels aloud. The orchid she bought me from the gift shop lived for what felt like a year.

It wasn't nearly as hard as I'd feared, getting my bag past the entrance, past a stern looking old English woman who only smiled after I'd handed her the money.

I take out the urn with my mum's ashes in it and try to think what to say. What can I say? I listen for voices, the voices of onlookers, and can't hear any. I do the deed silently, hearing a plane fly low overhead and knowing that the dust that I'm scattering here isn't a person, isn't my mum, though it was part of her once.

In another building, I find the conservatory full of carnivorous plants. There are dozens of them, but none that are purple and orange. I reach into my bag and take out the baby that came with me from Oxford. Quickly, I slip it in with the rest. I stand for as long as I dare to, thinking of Iris, Iris White, whoever she was, and wishing tomorrow was already over. Not that I'll be anywhere near when Iris's coffin is pushed into the crematorium, watched by friends, family and colleagues, none of them aware — at least hopefully, God help us — that inside it she's already ash, the coffin's weight coming not from her body, but from three of her plants.

Mr Parker wasn't keen on my plan, not at first, until I opened the door of the van and he smelt it. 'You're right about this, young man,' he said, sipping air through his teeth. 'Your stepdad could be in a spot of trouble over this.' He seemed very interested in my other cargo, my stowaway plants, especially my orchid. He said his wife kept a hothouse.

I held my breath as we carried the coffin in, not to the morgue or the chapel — into a shed out the back. It was dark in there, full of dusty utensils. Mr Parker closed the door on her and locked it. I wanted to see her again before going, but knew it was better I didn't.

The door of the conservatory opens, and a group of schoolchildren file in. Walking on, I take my mobile out of my pocket to call Corey, my brother in Cornwall, to find out how long the drive is, from London to there. Before I can look up his number, the phone vibrates. The Dr Who theme plays, and I think back to Robin, back to the van, to this whole odd adventure I've had with three people I might never see again.

It's the old man calling. Nobody else. I let the tune play.

ANGUS

'You didn't need to let me win.'

Beads of sweat trickle down his chest. He is pale and doughy and almost hairless. I am tall, hirsute and still faintly tanned from years in the sun. She knew both these bodies. Knew them in the Old Testament sense. Loved them, enveloped them, moulded herself to them. But surely — the thought is out, childish and ignoble, before I can stop it — preferred mine...

'I didn't.'

Sometimes I call him Solly to wind him up, put him off his stroke as we racket around the court. He hates it. 'I'm Sol,' he says. 'Solomon.' The solemn one.

But not today. We played silently, fiercely, as if honouring something unspoken. Possibly unspeakable. Time will tell.

'Come on, Angus.'

'No, really.' It was true. Today it was true.

I could hardly have cried off after that phone call. Despite having had a week to prepare for it, albeit possibly the worst week of my life, it was not my finest hour. I readily admit it. But now part of me's curious, curious to know what he feels — if he feels anything. Of course, I condoled again as we met in the changing room. He shook his head and muttered something about being fine. His body language said 'not now, not today', though his voice said another thing. Now I look at him through the steam and feel suddenly breathless at the absurdity of our being here together — even though we've been here countless times before. Me and Solomon. Two halves of her life.

I grip the bench. It comes at me in waves, sends my innards crashing through the floor. For the first few days I was numb, disbelieving. Now I'm riding choppy waters. And part of me, inexplicably, wants him in this fragile craft alongside me, companion in grief. Also wants to shake him, shout at him: have you *any idea* what you — we — have lost?

Some days I feel as if I'm fragmenting. All these parts of me. The one that's equally curious to know what he knows. That thinks: if he has the slightest inkling that for twenty-five years he has been cuckolded by his squash partner, then today of all days I will see it in his eyes.

Even through this steam.

And I can't.

The children – her children, his children... our children. This journey they've been on. Not that she was on it with them, not in any real sense, most emphatically not. But the places, our places... When Stella first told me I felt violated, ransacked. Only for a moment or two, though. It's probably what I would have done too, given the chance. Later I almost laughed at the thought of Robin interrogating Stella as the prig Richard fell apart. Wondering if he might have the nous to figure it all out for himself...

Wretched game of squash. I'm not sure this weekly game is going to be sustainable. Tonight, whenever I looked at Angus, all I could see was Robin. Miserably, nothing was said between us. If only it had been, but I, well, we, were too cowardly. Butternuts squash. Yet the unsaid was everywhere, even in our playing. Angus, who is always ruthless on the squash court, didn't have the heart to win tonight, and kept feigning failed shots to keep me in rallies. So now we have our own RD Laing-style knotted relationship — I know that he knows, and he knows that I know that he knows, and I know that he knows that I know that he knows that I know, and so on *ad desperandum*.

It's raining outside. Runnels of water spill down the window in the gloom. I stare at the glass. It's a mirror. Window pain.

Why do I still love you, Iris? It's a curse. For all that, God knows, I had manifold faults, I'm not sure you deserve my continuing love. There. I've said it, at last. I sure as hell didn't have yours, did I, for very long?

It would be simple, too simple, to pin it all on my reluctance to have children. It wasn't even an outright refusal, just not what I was looking for at that stage. I needed more time, that's all. You could have talked me into it, like women have done through the ages. But not you. You took yourself off the pill and got yourself pregnant. I should have realised. Already our love life had cooled by that point, and your sudden ardour should have made me suspicious, except that I was too keen to see it as us having got past a bad patch.

It was symptomatic, though, wasn't it, Iris? More than the deception was the lack of respect. Your plants taking over the house, soil all over my books and clothes, notes on the kitchen table to let me know you'd gone off mushroom hunting in the New Forest, back on Tuesday. Except it turned out to be Thursday.

So when were you ever going to tell me? About getting pregnant I mean? Why did you make me have to ask you? More disrespect. You made me resent my own son before he was born. What hope did Richard and I have? And then competing for his attention from the moment he arrived, usurping my place, like he's continued to do for over thirty years. I get furious with him, but I should be furious with you.

And still, still, I longed for you, believed I could win you back, thought my silence and complicity might give you the time you needed. Not realising then that crevasses in ice only deepen.

Do you remember when I was so taken with Thoreau, in my early idealistic days? Do you recall me reading out some of his famous quotes? Do you remember 'The price of anything is the amount of life you exchange for it'?

By that reckoning, I'm still mortgaged up to the hilt.

Day 11

TUESDAY

ROBIN

So Bill, time you and I had a little chat.

I've spent the morning hanging around the funeral parlour while Father finalises arrangements for tomorrow's Sombre Event. Now I'm standing in the street outside with my phone in my hand and Bill's number on the screen. I'm pretty sure pressing 'Call' will open a catering-sized can of worms, but better that than the bollocks and duplicity that got the White family into this mess in the first place.

Four rings then:

'Angus Fleming.'

It's not him. Christ, don't tell me it's all an innocent mistake...

'Er, is Bill there?'

'No. I'm afraid you must have the wrong number.'

Wait. The name and that voice are vaguely familiar. Middle-aged at a guess, Scottish but with a touch of the transatlantic. It's times like this I wish my memory was intact. I dive in quickly before he can hang up.

'It's Robin White here.'

Silence. Has he bolted?

'Hello?'

'Ah Robin, yes. I, er, heard about your mother. I'm so very sorry for you all. And your father, how is he? Is he bearing up?'

Hmm. Clearly the *right* number. Whoever Angus is he's remarkably well informed about my family. And if the growing feeling in my gut is anything to go by that's only to be expected. I've started so I'd better finish.

'I've just left him. He's got calls to make before tomorrow. Anyway, I found this number in Iris's phone and I thought Bill and I should talk. I suspect we've quite a bit in common. Iris, for example.'

Another short silence. Then, 'Indeed. I've been wondering if I might hear from you.'

'So... you *are* Bill? After all?'

'In a manner of speaking, yes. I am Bill. And I imagine you have questions you would like to ask me.'

You imagine right. 'Let me guess. You and Iris had a relationship, perhaps for many years, and my father doesn't know. Or rather he chooses not to. Am I right?'

'Yes, Robin. You are right.'

There's a note in his voice that says he's holding something back. Interesting: Angus/Bill is waiting to see what I know – exactly what I'd do in his situation. I take a chance.

'But that's not all...?'

Long pause. 'Not... entirely.'

'So?'

'Well...' and suddenly I know what's coming. I get that sick feeling as he continues.

'... you see, Robin, I loved your mother enormously. For a very long time. Nearly thirty years in fact. And the thing is ...'

'Solomon's not my father.' There. I've said it.

'No.'

'And you are?'

'Yes, Robin. I am.'

Fuck. In fact, FUCK. That's what you call coming clean. This thing I've sort of known all along but never admitted. I blurt out the first thing that comes into my head.

'So... why didn't Mother dump him and the two of you do it properly? Wouldn't you have been happier?'

'Robin, there's nothing I would have loved more in the world. But life's not always quite that straightforward. We thought it best for everyone to keep it quiet and try to limit the possible – um – damage.' He sighs. 'I've... often wondered if you knew.'

'Well, I had my doubts about Father – or rather Sol as I'll have to start thinking of him.' *Can't say I'm too bothered. Sol's always been a prize wanker.* 'So yes, I suppose you've only confirmed what I suspected.'

'Look, Robin, I realise this is a great deal for you to take on board, especially with your mother gone. There will be plenty of time to talk in due course, once everyone's got over the – shock. But meanwhile, I gather the funeral's tomorrow. I would very much like to attend – if it won't create difficulties, that is...?'

'You're coming tomorrow? Fine by me. See you there. And don't worry, I won't say anything untoward. Not in my interests is it? Not in anyone's interests at this late stage.'

The nanosecond I hang up I remember who Angus Fleming is. He's Sol's long-time squash partner. *Of course.* Wow, so that's my real dad? Explains a lot. I'm reeling a little here – as you do when you discover a major error in your apparent parentage – but I think I might have come out on top in this little deal. From what I can remember Angus is the least uncool of my parents' – well, ex-parents' – friends. Some sort of former music biz guy as I recall. Looked like he'd been around a bit. Iris could have done a lot worse, and so could I.

ANGUS

Takes one to know one.

It was in his voice. Beneath the bluster a trace of urgency, need, hunger. I heard it. No one else would have.

We're creatures of excess, my son and I. The only difference being that I've learned to curb mine.

It troubled her. Of course it did. She never said it directly, though the reproach was there: *your* genes. Well, we'll see if he has *my* resolve. He certainly has her brain. It should be a winning combination. Give him time. It took me ten years of excess for the penny to drop. Ten years of the kind of debauchery that only the music industry can offer, the kind that would have made Robin's eyes water. A lost – though profitable – decade that ended in the needless death of the woman I thought was my soulmate. Until, that is, his mother came along.

One day, perhaps, I'll tell him about the Nashville years. But then again, perhaps not... One day, perhaps, I'll tell him about the Balmore years, about what all these places he's been to in the last week really meant to us.

How strange. I lose her and in the losing, our bargain – that I will never acknowledge him to anyone other than her – is cancelled. So I gain him. And it is a gain, believe me, whatever one might think of his behaviour, his attitude to life, his – habits. He is *my son*. My son *with* Iris. And I know that what we share is bred in the bone.

But how will he come to think of me?

I'm selfish and unreliable as only someone who has lived on his own for nearly three decades can be. I consider myself in a modest way a *bon viveur*. I am even a connoisseur of certain things, skirts for example, of which I am still, I confess, an incurable, though these days largely harmless, chaser. I am also, contradictory as it might sound, a romantic, capable of fierce loyalty and devotion – as I like to think his mother would have attested. He'll make his own judgment of these things in time.

More immediately though – and this he'll certainly like – I have a mews house in Notting Hill and a timeshare in Antigua, a healthy portfolio, and a decent stake in a small independent distillery on Speyside – the place where I grew up, whence also my connection with David Mackintosh and Balmore. I'm lucky — when it comes to money, at least. Always have been. The royalties continue to roll in, though I can't claim any real credit for them. I am — or was — an opportunist, a twenty-something Scotsman on the make who had the wit and brass neck to draft a couple of good, watertight contracts at the right moment.

So, a carrot perhaps, for Robin to clean up his act and make someone proud of him.

Though how we negotiate Solomon, I'm not quite sure...

I can't quite believe the change in Robin. Here we are, driving to the chapel of rest to make final arrangements with the undertaker. We're thrown together as the most unlikely funeral arrangers, and he is significantly more together and connected to the real world than I have known him for a decade. He seems, well, purposeful. Although neither of us has mentioned it to this point, I think there is a mutual, vicious pleasure, hideous to admit to, in knowing that Richard has lost the plot. It's in the air between us, but not commented on, until Robin makes a reference to it. He's clearly keen to get my take on it all, but he's being unusually subtle and sensitive.

'I have to say, Father, it's a relief to be in this vehicle with you, rather than that fucking nonsense van that brother Richard had us cavorting around the country in.'

I pick my words with care. 'It sounded like quite a mission he was set on.'

'It was a folly, a bloody Shakespearean tragedy. He's like King fucking Lear, he's gone mad with his knowledge.'

'Oh?' I now know what the knowledge is of course, but it's geological knowledge, compacted layers of deposit, and I don't know how much they have managed to chip away at. Out of the corner of my eye, I spot Robin wince. He's realised that he shouldn't have gone down this route. What was discovered on tour should stay on tour, he of all people should know that. He changes tack.

'Hey, Father, I owe you an apology. We were shabby to you. I can't just hide behind Richard being a complete dick. I could have done better. And I didn't.'

I'm moved by this. What a shame that it takes Iris's death to create a father and son moment between us. Well, I say that, but that's not right is it? Adopted father and son? But I didn't adopt him, did I? Cuckolded father and son? What's the relationship here?

'Thank you, Robin. That's decent. I won't pretend it wasn't shitty, because it was. But hey, there are lots of apologies due, and they start with me, and the kind of father I've been.'

There's a tension so deep in the car that I know that Robin knows, without anything having to be said. We come up to a red light, and I turn to look at him. He can't look at me, he stares fixedly straight ahead. Suddenly it's even more obvious. I see Angus. It's the mirror image of only seeing Robin during my squash match, like one of those optical illusions where you stare and stare, and then, for no obvious reason, see a picture that was hidden to you up to that point.

But my instinct tells me that he doesn't know quite as much as me, and I'm not going to tell him if he doesn't pursue it. Just like I'm not going to call Angus on it. I never confronted Iris, and she was the person I should have had the conversation with. If Robin asks, we'll talk about it. If Angus confesses, then it will be out in the open. But I'm not going to be the one to light the blue touchpaper. I've lost a son through this debacle, in fact I may have lost two. Inexplicably, and in spite of what I thought after the squash match, I don't want to lose Angus as well, even if it turns out that he was the worst kind of friend. In the most diabolical fashion, like my own version of Stockholm syndrome, he's part of my living connection to Iris, and I'm not ready to give up on that just yet. And maybe, just maybe, not being prepared to give up is going to be what saves me.

REBECCA

Rebecca White @rebwhite   2m
Anyone got a nice black coat, size 8?

Day 12

WEDNESDAY

ANGUS

I have to go today. To prove to Robin who I am. And to Solomon who I am not.

At the back of my bathroom cabinet I keep a small, now rather elderly, stash of essential medicaments. You never knew that, did you, *mo chree*? But old habits die hard. Twenty minutes ago I popped a downer. Now the anxiety is dulling.

Mo chree. You loved it when I called you that. My heart. The Gaelic gilding our passion. *Gra mo chree. Love of my heart.*

My fingers fumble with the clasp of the bracelet you gave me all those years ago. Deep coppery gold, a chain of slender links, delicate but just masculine enough. You bought it for me to replace the one I lost, even though I knew you disapproved. I only ever wore it when we were together. Perhaps after today I'll always wear it. Perhaps I'll never wear it again. I don't know.

Bought in the days when you found me impossibly exotic, the brash young widower with the louche, wild turkey scent of Nashville still on him. And I found you – subtle. Subtle and beautiful in an extraordinary and understated way that I had never encountered before. Like something discovered under moss. Everything about you made the world I'd come from seem crass and lumpen, most of all your knowledge... You taught me to read and learn. I taught you to live.

I feed the links through the cuffs, then hold up my wrist and shake gently so the bracelet slides down inside my shirtsleeve.

Yes. We were lucky, you and I. It was truly a rare thing, this fire kindled from opposite matter, that burned so strongly, so brightly all those years. Hardest of all, the fact that it would be burning still if only I hadn't been held up. If only you hadn't felt let down. If only we hadn't rowed that night. If only I had loved you better still. If only you hadn't loved so much – so much that your poor bloody heart burst...

If. If. If. There are too many in life.

I know one thing. I cannot, will not live with If. And you must help me, wherever you are. Remind me every day that we were the lucky ones. Help me carry your loveliness in my heart till the end, a force for everything that is good in my life and the world.

Oh, Iris, Iris, *mo chree, gra mo chree...*

ROBIN

Is it wrong to say I like her better now she's dead?

Finding the real Iris has been strangely therapeutic. The last thing I want to acknowledge is any learning or growing as a result of our little adventure, but I can't deny Richard and I are closer. I mean, he's even lent me a suit for this afternoon. It's awful beyond belief, but the point is he offered it; two weeks ago Rich wouldn't have lent me so much as someone else's sweaty sock.

So here I am, back in the flat, as if the last fortnight never happened. The living room curtains are still closed, the rubbish is still waiting to be taken out, the lavatory is still... well, it's as it was. No sign of Mental Mark either, thank God.

Adie smiles as I drop my bag. 'How was Scotland? Thought you'd be back last week. I even bought you a Twix to celebrate your return.'

'Really?' I'm starving. I do love Adie.

'Yeah, then I got the munchies and ate it.' Oh well.

'Never mind fella, it's the thought that counts. But yeah, things took a bit longer than we anticipated, hence my delayed return. Quite amazing, the skeletons in the White family closets. I'm starting to see myself in a whole new light. I'll tell you about it sometime.'

He passes me a stubby little joint. I don't mind if I do. In fact, I do mind if I don't. As I take a pull I see Adie eying the cheap suit bag Rich gave me to protect Burton's finest.

'What's with the whistle?'

'Mother's funeral. She died, remember? We're burying her this afternoon. Gotta look the part.'

'I don't suppose I could borrow it for my forthcoming appearance at Southwark?'

Ordinarily I'd have said yes without a thought but now...

'Thing is, it's not mine to lend. It belongs to Brother Richard.'

Adie nods sagely. They met once. 'Dick by name, dick by nature.'

'The very same. I'll ask him, though. You never know. He's not quite the git he was.'

And so on and so forth. But even as we're talking I'm thinking that none of us knew who she really was. And now, well, now we know too much. The thing is, keeping up a double life for quarter of a century, well, you've got to tip your hat to that kind of commitment. She silently stuck two fingers up at the world and went her own sweet way. No excuses and no explanations. That's something I can almost understand.

The consolations of poetry. I've been reading a lot of it in the last twenty-four hours, it seems to help. *Staying alive*, as the book says. At times this limited achievement doesn't seem much to thank anyone for. Surrounded by my family, I feel detached. But I think of Mum with an intensity that I haven't felt for a long time. In a strange way she needed to die to come fully alive for me.

I remember a poem I'd read in translation. It begins: 'Whatever flower you are, you are a flower of beauty.' Tears form in my eyes, trickle down my face, but I feel no need to hide them. Julia sees and holds my hand.

We sit in the back of the funeral car that follows the hearse with Mum's coffin inside. All around the coffin are laid bunches of irises. Julia has done this well, it's her idea. I wish I loved her as much as Mum. Opposite us in the quiet car sit my dad, Robin and Rebecca. What a ragtaggle crew we make. Dad looks every inch the professional mourner in black suit, black tie and white shirt. He lacks only the top hat – perhaps he should borrow one from the chap sitting in the front seat? Next to Dad, Robin has dressed with his own nod towards convention. In a black shirt and my suit that doesn't quite fit him. The orange socks are a bit too visible below the turn-ups of the trousers. Rebecca seems agitated but she might just be conscious that her coat is a few sizes too large for her.

Julia looks immaculate.

I look down at myself. Scrubbed up and uncomfortable in a suit with a heavy overcoat. No flower of beauty me.

Perhaps I could have been a poet. But no, I'm only a reader of poetry. Perhaps I am what I was always meant to be. A doctor, not one who dispenses short poems on prescription pads but the kind who scribbles '100mg, morning and night'. A family doctor. But I could be a better doctor.

The car slows to a pace that can only be called funereal as we pass through the gates of the cemetery. Everything is slow and quiet and ordered. Even Robin. There's a drizzle falling, rivulets of rain run down the window, from drop to drop. Outside the scene is full of crosses, crosses everywhere, made of stone. Monumental slabs with the names of the dead, marble ornaments for the more ostentatious, even statues of the

Virgin Mary for the devout. Not us. I see a building like a stone beach house topped by the figure of an angel, a white one, and the words 'Family Mausoleum of the Birkett Family' carved into the frame. Ours could be in the shape of a white van with dark wings on either side.

Julia mistakes my half-smile for bravery and squeezes my hand again. We are here, at the brick building that is the crematorium. As we get out of the limousine and walk towards the portico, we are each greeted by the clergyman who mutters his kind of consolation. It's not poetry.

I'm inclined to hate the service but find it moving, despite myself. Despite the priest's obvious lack of knowledge of my mum he at least gets all the names right. In the case of my mum she's plumped up for death with the full 'Iris Virginia White'. I weep when the furnace door opens and her coffin slides out of sight. The curtain is pulled closed, and she is gone, finally she is gone.

I regret the trip in the van. It was a terrible mistake, my mistake. But I was trying to do what felt right, even if it turned out wrong. Forgive me, Mum.

We file out as the Beatles sing 'Dear Prudence' to us all. Rebecca chose it, having got to like the song on Mum's phone. Outside the sun gently nudges aside the clouds, but it's only for a moment. I want to wander a little in these grounds where daffodils are still in bright bloom among the dormant rose bushes and the dark trees. A blackbird sings, beckoning me away from the gathering chatter of the funeral guests. I see Stella is there, even Angus, but I have no real wish to speak with them.

I look at the metal plaques on the stone kerb of the gardens, name after name, a curving line of deceased humanity. All gone, all remembered to varying degrees. I come to the most recent plaque:

WILL WATSON

1942 – 2013

Sweet darling man

I feel an unexpected kinship though no one is likely to use such words about me. What should we say about Mum when our time for remembrance by plaque arrives? *She was a human being and we loved her.*

Would that be true? I see Robin and Rebecca looking cold, wet and miserable; Julia stares anxiously at me over my dad's shoulder as he talks to Stella. I know I loved her. I still do. I could be a better human being, especially if I tried. Physician, heal thyself, as the pompous priest might tell me, given the chance. What do you think, Mum? Rain meanders down from my desert scalp to the tips of my nose and chin. I stroll back to the group, thinking about the advantages of growing a beard.

A death's not a time to be critical of the person who has died. Better to turn the critical light on those still living. If something's wrong, try to do something about the living. Especially yourself. It is Richard that you mourn for. Doctor. Brother. Father, son and holy ghost.

Here is what I know about love and life.

Love has leaked through the cracks in my lives like a darkness. I couldn't contain it. I couldn't contain my life. How dangerous it was to live in this way.

And now my living behind me gaping like a broken seed. Just when I thought I might find room at last for everyone I loved.

Grief is the opposite of love. It's the negative image. It's the black hole that's left in our lives when we lose someone. This grief of theirs is about a love of theirs, about a love for me and about the loss of what they thought they knew. And I grieve too, for them, but also, for me and the life I never lived. All I wanted to do was live, really live. I just wanted to live.

REBECCA

From: Rebecca White
To: Iris White
Subject: OMFG

I know we've kind of said goodbye properly now mum, but I'm in SHOCK. And there's no one else I can talk to. It was on the news – H has been ARRESTED. In France, with one of his students. Yes, another one. And she's younger than me. At least you're not going to say I told you so. That could have been ME all over the TV. What was I thinking mum??? They were at some countryside hotel under false names. Any of that sound familiar? In the paper it said they were caught because of a tip-off from a mystery woman called Fleur. Who was she? How could she have known??? Anyway, I'm through with love you'll be pleased to know. Just want things to get back to normal. Some kind of normal. Probably stay with Richard and Jules for a while. Dad needs some time. Love you mum. Bye for now.

> **Where are you?**

AFTERWORD

by Stuart Delves, Jamie Jauncey and John Simmons

Now that you have read this story, we thought you might like to know how a collective novel comes to be written. The clue, of course, lies in the use of We. This novel does not have one author but fifteen different ones. That makes it unusual, if not unique. How did fifteen writers collaborate to produce a work of narrative fiction?

The three of us writing this afterword – yes, with this book everything happens in multiples – decided in 2004 to begin running creative writing courses for writers in the business world. So much business writing is dull and unimaginative, but it need not be. We wanted to use literary techniques – drawn from stories, novels, poetry – to help people become more creative writers at work. One of us, John Simmons, wrote a book called *Dark Angels* advocating the philosophy we apply in our courses. We decided to name them after that book.

The courses worked (and still do). One led to another, one level to another, and still people continued to ask 'What next?' Feeling we had nothing left to impart to our more advanced students, we wondered if instead we could continue the journey in the spirit of exploration, learning alongside our fellow travellers, rather than teaching them. So we created a first collaborative project, an exhibition called *Other Worlds* at Oxford's Story Museum in 2012. Twenty writers took part, each working with a visual artist. But then the 'What next?' question arose again, and this time the three of us wondered if we could bring a group of writers together to create a work of fiction.

There's no handy guide called *How to Write a Collective Novel* so we had to come up with our own plan. We felt it would be impossible to tell a linear narrative with fifteen writers trying to achieve the same, consistent tone of voice. So we looked at novels with multiple voices: William Faulkner's *As I Lay Dying*, Matthew Kneale's *English Passengers*, and David Mitchell's *Cloud Atlas*. *As I Lay Dying* was of particular interest because it was written from the first-person viewpoints of all the different characters in the story. This approach solved our problem. Each writer would take on the distinctive voice of a different character and the diversity would be part of the richness of the book.

Invitations went out to join us over a long weekend and a dozen enthusiastic replies followed. In mid-March 2013 a group of fifteen writers (including the three of us) — from Scotland, England, Denmark and Sweden — gathered at Balavil, a large country house in the Scottish Highlands where we were wonderfully looked after by our hosts, Allan and Marjorie Macpherson-Fletcher. We had planned it as a spring weekend, but this year winter was reluctant to let go its grip. Sitting round log fires added to the atmosphere and, as expected, the house itself proved a spur to our imaginations, the sense of place enriching the experience we shared as writers. In the novel, Balavil has mutated into Balmore, similar but different in many ways from each other.

Prior to the weekend the three of us had agreed a story outline that allowed each of the fifteen characters to play their part in telling the story. (Coincidentally, the number of voiced characters in Faulkner's novel was also fifteen.) The outline was a simple two-page synopsis, inspired by Faulkner's story but transferring period and location from the deep south of America in the early twentieth century to Scotland and England in 2013: a woman dies suddenly and mysteriously in a Scottish country house; as her three children take her coffin back to London by road, visiting her favourite places along the way, her secret life is gradually revealed.

Having assigned each writer a character, the main focus of that wintry weekend was to flesh out the characters with names, back stories, personalities and motivations. As we came to know our alter egos and the role each might play at different points along the journey, we added our thoughts to the storyline outlined on flipcharts. By the end of the weekend we had each tested our character's credibility by writing a piece in his or her voice.

We also had a plot that now had much more detail and had branched out in unexpected ways as characters had got together in small groups to explore their relationships and possible interventions. What happens where and when, who takes the floor at a given time to tell the story, and so on — the process was probably closer to that of developing a play or film script than a traditional novel.

Following the weekend, John sifted through the mass of notes and flipcharts to create a detailed story plan that listed day-by-day what would happen and who would tell the story at each point. Then it was over to the members of the cast to write — from Iris at the start of Day 1 through to Rebecca at the end of Day 12.

Of course there were hitches along the way. People grew attached to their characters and developed clear pictures of their idiosyncrasies. Like film-makers we had to keep alert to issues of continuity, of characters getting out of sequence, or speaking out of character in reported dialogue, or simply being described as wearing clothes that were not in the heads of their 'owners'. But, considering there were fifteen of us working separately, these issues were relatively few and easy to smooth away in the editing process.

Claire Bodanis had volunteered as our project manager, as well as writing Philip, the young guest at Balmore. Claire marshalled us all and held us to our agreed timetable, and where it slipped it was no fault of hers. In the days before email this would have been an unbearably protracted, if not impossible, process.

We had left Balavil with a flipchart full of possible titles, for example *Dying and Lying* — as that's what the book is about. A few weeks later Stuart suggested *As I Died Lying*, tipping his hat to the Faulkner novel. We all thought this was clever and we funded the book through Unbound with that title. But when we came to read the first full draft, the theme of relationships with mother seemed to be everywhere. So we went back to one of our original titles, *Keeping Mum*.

Collaborating on *Keeping Mum* has been an extraordinary experience for all of us involved. We hope the pleasure of reading it has been equal to the pleasure of writing it.

SUBSCRIBERS

Unbound is a new kind of publishing house. Our books are funded directly by readers. This was a very popular idea during the late eighteenth and early nineteenth centuries. Now we have revived it for the internet age. It allows authors to write the books they really want to write and readers to support the writing they would most like to see published.

The names listed below are of readers who have pledged their support and made this book happen. If you'd like to join them, visit: unbound.co.uk.

Michael Abrahams	Christopher Bland
John Ainley	Gemma Blencowe
John Alexander	Paul Blezard
Rob Allen	David Bodanis
Tony Allen	Annabelle Bonus
John Allert	Mark Bowers
Lindsey Appleby	Elena Bowes
Matt Armstrong	Rosel Boycott
Nick Asbury	Sophie Brand
Zuzu Aspen	Robert Brandt
Heather Atchison	Richard W H Bray
Emmajane Avery	Sophie Brodie
Will Awdry	Ian Brownhill
Neil Baker	Meike Brunkhorst
Jayne Barrett	Peregrine Bryant
Alex Batchelor	Gareth Buchaillard-Davies
Larisa Bernstein	Rosie Buckman
Dean Beswick	Ali & Tony Burns
Julia Bindman	Judith Cair
Andy Bird	Steve Cameron
Annie Blaber	Xander Cansell
Stuart Blake	Nick Capaldi

Ezri Carlebach
David Carroll
Jason Carter
Cedric Carton
Peter Castelli
Sam Chesterton
Lorna Christie
Alison M Clark
Alexandra Clarke
Louisa Clarke
Martin Clarkson
Peter Clifton
Ali Coates
Melanie Cochran
Philippa Cochrane
Eliza Cockerell
Richard Cohen
Victoria Coleing
Andrea Coleman
Stevyn Colgan
Gillian Colhoun
Robert Colvile
Martha Cook
Jo-anne Cooper
Pat Cooper
Allan Corduner
Clare Craig
Richard Cripps
Robin Cunninghame Graham
Charles d'Arcy-Irvine
Dark Angels
Jonathan Dart

Christopher Davenport
Melissa Davis
Oliver Davy
Charlie Dawson
Susan Deacon
Jan Dekker
Hamish Delves
John Dodds
Julie Doel
Rebecca Dowman
Roger Duerden
Neil Duffy
Rebecca Eames
Vincent Eames
Fiona Egglestone
Iain Ellwood
Robert England
Hayley Equi
Alan Evans
Verity Evans
Aurora Evans-Kleijn
David Falcon
Julius Falcon
Sarah Farley
Joe Ferry
Janet Fogg
Mark Forsyth
Essie Fox
Adam Fransella
Melissa Frost
Hilary Gallo
Elizabeth Garner

David Giles
Kimberly Girard
Salena Godden
Alison Gold
Paul Goodban
Janet Gordon
Wendy Gordon
Voula Grand
John Grant
Sam Gray
Chris Green
Chris Gribble
Angus Grundy
Tim Hall
Charlotte Halliday
David Hampton
Sally Harper
Simon Harper
Fiona Hart
Susannah Hart
Joy Hawley
Andy Hayes
Martin Hayward
Martin Hennessey
Henzteeth
E O Higgins
Kelly Hill
Sarah Hill
Sarah L. Hill
Andrew Hoddinott
Gill Hodge
Tom Hodgkinson

Anita Holford
Graeme Holland
Lindsay Horberry
Roger Horberry
Jules Horne
Jo Howard
Andrew Hulme
Laura Humble
Tony Hunt
Aurora Jauncey
Jamie Jauncey
Sarah Jauncey
Simon Jauncey
Christoffer Jensen
Edward Johnstone
Kerri Jones
Wendy Jones
Maida Kaiser
Nadav Kander
Paul Keilthy
Trudi Kent
Gordon Kerr
Rachael Kerr
Edna Kissmann
Richard Koenig
Debbie Kohn
Deborah Kohn
Jennifer and Peter Larsen
Magnus Larsson
Jimmy Leach
Adrienne and Brian Lee
Jon Lee

Martin Lee
Monika Lehner
Elen Lewis
Jane Lindsay
Gyles Lingwood
Hillier London
Rob Luijten
Simon Luke
Miranda Luxford
Johan Maack
Douglas McCabe
Louise McCabe
Elisabeth McIntosh
Miranda McKearney
Andrew Mackenzie
Shirley Mackenzie
Caroline Mckeown
Allan Macpherson-Fletcher
Jo Macsween
Esther Maughan McLachlan
David May
Anne Miller
Justine Miller
Andy Milligan
Ronald Mitchinson
Kim Møller-Elshøj
Alison Morris
Daniel Mudford of Balham
Damian Mullan
Paul Murphy
Bob Mytton
Paul Neale

Amanda Nelson
Jacqui Nelson
Karina Nelson
Susan Nickalls
Michelle Nicol
Paul Nixon
Mark Noad
Isobel Noble
Daniel Nolan
Karin Nordborg
Tamara O'Brien
Aaron O'Donnell
John O'Donnell
Cate O'Kane
Anders Östling
Åsa Pallier
Max Pallier Gustafsson
Richard Palmer
Isabella Park
Nick Parker
Ian Parkinson
Kate Pasterfield
Gillian Paull
Richard Pelletier
Dan Peters
Justin Pollard
Mark Polson
Jean Polwarth
Barclay Price
Scott Purdon
Rebecca Quayle
Luisa Ramazzotti

Jeanette Ramsden
Julie Randles
Emily Ranneby
Anne Redstone
Mark Redstone
Jane Reeve
Manfred Reuters
Luci Reynolds
Philip Riddle
Kasper Riis
James Robertson
Barbara Roddam
Ben Romans
Anna Rowlands
Tomos Rowlands
Jennifer Ryan
Suleyman Sanik
Jon Sayers
Brian Schildt
Caroline Schmitz
Tom Scott
Tom Scott
Sandra Seru
Faye Sharpe
Benn Shepherd
Dan Shepherd
Mary Shepherd
Ada Simmons
Aimee Simmons
Cari Simmons
Jessie Simmons
John Simmons

Linda Simmons
Nicolas Sireau
Nicola Sloan
Tim Smit
Anna Smith
Shaun Smith
John Solly
Frances and John Sorrell
Olivia Sprinkel
Robert Stanford
Matt Stephens
Ruby Stevenson
Gordon Stewart
John Stewart
Maggie Strasser
Julian Stubbs
Andrew Sunnucks
Kay Syrad
Rob Taylor
Fiona Thompson
Lizzy Tinley
Rachel Tofts
Sian Tomos
Cat Totty
Colin Turner
Julie Turner
Kathrin Turner
Falmouth University
Elise Valmorbida
Michael Van der Gucht
Zoe van Zwanenberg
Anelia Varela

Mark Vent

Cecilia Vinell

Erica Wagner

Jennifer Walker

Esther Wallace

Vivien Wallace

John Walsh

Marcus and Sally Walsh

Jonathan Waring

George Watkins

Jackie Watkins

James Watkins

Mark Watkins

Teresa Watkins

Corrie Watson

Will Watson

Sue Wells

Alan Whelan

Ferne Whipp

Samantha Wilkinson

Rob Williams

Joanna Wilmot

Claire Wilson

Keeley Wilson

Guy Windsor

Isabel Windsor

Maxine Windsor

Michaela Windsor

Rebecca Windsor

Richard Windsor

Sharn Woodgate

Mo Woodward

Alison Woolven

Andy York

Penny Young

Nicolas Zekulin

Spinoza Pro is an award-winning face designed by New York-based art director, illustrator, toy designer and novelist Max Phillips over the course of eleven years. Described as 'an elegant workhorse', the face was named after Dutch philosopher Benedict de Spinoza, whose work laid the foundations for eighteenth-century Enlightenment and modern biblical criticism (philosopher Georg Wilhelm Friedrich Hegel said, 'you are either a Spinozist or not a philosopher at all'). Spinoza is credited, in simple terms, with helping people to see the world more clearly – hence the type's tributary title.

Gill Sans was designed by English sculptor, typeface designer, stonecutter and printmaker Eric Gill, and takes inspiration from Edward Johnston's typeface for the London Underground, on which Gill had worked while apprenticed to Johnston himself. Gill Sans was later chosen as the official typeface of the London and North Eastern Railway; it was famously used on the classic rail posters of the twenties and, later, the iconic Penguin books jacket designs.